Bree T. Donovan and Linda Prefontaine

Steve Prefontaine

– Rocketman –

This book is dedicated to Ray and Elfriede Prefontaine;
partners, parents and teachers who loved greatly.
Thank You.

Reference Materials:

Pre - The Story of America's Greatest Running Legend, Steve Prefontaine.
Tom Jordan. Published by Rodale Press.

The Eugene Register Guard, The Oregonian. Newspapers, Eugene, Oregon.
The Coos Bay World. Newspaper, Coos Bay, Oregon

Fire on the Track - The Steve Prefontaine Story.
Chambers Productions, Eugene Oregon.

ABC Sports coverage of the 1972 Olympic 5000 meter race, Munich, Germany.

Acknowledgments

To all the readers who will journey through the pages of this book - the young and the forever young at heart - I hope you find meaning in the story of Pre. I hope you will think of him every time you face a challenge and, win or lose, you will proceed with pride because you did your best.

Please bear with me, as I have some very good people that I would like to acknowledge. We all have "cheerleaders" in our lives, and I'd sure like to thank mine.

Working on this book has been one of the most joyful experiences of my life. I have many wonderful people to thank, most especially Steve Prefontaine. I have no doubt his light and legacy will be circling the universe for a long time to come - partly because of his great, big spirit, and partly because of all those who love him and keep his flame glowing.

I'm grateful to my family. As with most, we are a silly, crazy, and loving lot. I too could never forget where I came from, and wouldn't want to. Thanks, guys! A special "shout-out" to Breanna and Kristina - always dream big!

To my friends who put up with all my doubts and dark days, and saw me through to the other side; for all those long conversations which included coffee, ice cream and chocolate. Thank you!

To my editor, friend, and a most favorite writer, JJ Beazley - you are truly unselfish, and I am very fortunate to know and learn from you. Thank you for your wise and generous spirit.

To my co-workers at CONTACT, ya'll have more heart than most. You stood by me and then some. Who'd have thought it would be a feisty runner from Coos Bay, Oregon that held the key?!

Tom Jordan, the writer of *Pre-The Story of America's Greatest Running Legend* and the man who so generously helped me, not only with his connections but by giving me permission to incorporate information from his book. I strongly encourage every Pre fan, and indeed anyone who aspires to be more, to read Tom's book.

For those special people in Coos Bay (most especially "The Coos Bay Kids"-Jay and Sy in particular!) and Eugene, "Pre's People" (some of whom are now scattered in different parts of Oregon and the country.) "Thank You" seems so small in return for all the time, memories and emotions you so generously shared with me. It's obvious how much Pre's relationships were based on mutual love and respect. I've learned from you, and I am humbled by you. *Every* voice in this book is special and extraordinary. I'm sure glad for phone cards!

Thanks to the University of Oregon's Daily Emerald and Marshfield High (Ma-Hi Times) newspapers for allowing me the liberty to use your names and be creative.

Also, many thanks to the people at the University of Oregon's Knight Library - especially the Reference dept!

Thank you to the administration of The Oregon State Penitentiary for helping me to gain information.

The Prefontaine Memorial Committee who every day keeps the flame burning – and puts up with all my e-mails.

Blossom Gulch School. Keep on running! Hope this helps!

ChildrenSong Choir. You amaze me. Thank you, Rick Ober for your excellent song arrangement.

Sara Charmé-Zane - for your fantastic vision and talent. Go get 'em at college!

Thank you to all the local media (in NJ and Coos Bay) who have been so supportive of this project. Thank you for bringing it to the communities.

Speaking of media...Tracy Hickman of Hickman Communications, you are superb. You donated your time, talents and heart because you believed in the project and the necessity to spread the message of Pre. I'm glad for your cell phone too!

Chris Cline. You carry on the tradition of guts!

Brett Holtz. Nike should be darn happy to have you!

Last, but most certainly not least, Linda Prefontaine - my co-author - for your time, memories, critical eye and sense of humor. I'm so glad I got to know you as more than "Little Pre." Thanks too for taking my call last winter.

BTD

About the Authors:

Bree T. Donovan is an educator, social service provider and the author of several short works of fiction who lives in Oaklyn, New Jersey. She knows first hand the importance of Pre's imperative to never give up in the pursuit of ones dreams. It is because of Pre's amazing life and spirit that Bree now has the passion to write and share the message of the Gift with children of all ages.

Linda Prefontaine is an accomplished athlete in her own right as a well-respected tennis and racquetball player. Steve's younger sister makes her home in Eugene, Oregon. Linda manages her own company, Prefontaine Productions, which is committed to what she calls, "Pieces of Pre" bringing the story of her brother to both the old and new generation of fans. Linda has generously given many hours of her time as a consultant and fact checker for this project.

About the Illustrator:

Sara Charmé-Zane is a senior at Germantown Friends School. Sara has been visually rendering the world around her since the age of three. From ceramics and mosaics to drawing and painting, Sara's work mostly deals with people, exploring everything about their beautiful selves and their interactions with the artist, each other, and the greater world around them. She is also fascinated by the relationships that can be built between words and images. Living in Philadelphia, Pennsylvania with her family, Sara belongs to one evil cat and her awesome younger sister, Tali.

Whatever you can do, or dream you can, begin it. Boldness has genius, power, and magic in it.

- Goethe -

You have to wonder at times what you're doing out there. Over the years I've given myself a thousand reasons to keep running, but it always comes back to where it started. It comes down to self-satisfaction and a sense of achievement.

- Steve Prefontaine –

This story of Steve Prefontaine is told through the voice of Owen Morgan. Owen is a literary device - a fictitious character who represents real persons and places. Although the person of Owen did not exist, the people he interacts with and the places and events he recounts are true and real. The stories that Owen shares with you, the reader, are the stories of those people who knew and loved Steve Prefontaine and the people he loved. These are the chronicles of actual happenings through the perspective of those who knew Steve best.

Preface
Aquarius Rising

Coos Bay, Oregon can be downright cold and gloomy in the wintertime. The landscape is defined by great, deep woods, thick, muddy earth, and fishing boats ever patrolling the waters for a bountiful catch.

The folks of Coos Bay are as imbedded in their town as the old trees, and tough as weathered loggers. They are as invigorated by their sports as by a long walk in the woods on a crisp January day.

One particular day in January, the twenty-fifth to be exact, Steve Roland Prefontaine joined the ranks of proud Oregonians. The year was 1951.

There are those who believe the alignment of the stars predict the path of a person; maybe so, maybe not. Steve was born an Aquarius, the water carrier, entering a section of the world where fishermen and the tides are as central to the town's life blood as oxygen.

It is said that Aquarians are strong and attractive personalities. They are high-spirited and dynamic. Those born to this sign have depth of character, maintain strong beliefs and, above all else, they seek the truth.

Some people believe that the stars in the sky are the souls of those who have died. Fire and water, stars and destiny; there are many theories about these mystical forces. Close your eyes and imagine them right here among us. Yet they are very difficult to contain or understand totally. Each brings the world light, energy and a sense of wonder.

There are those who believe that some very unique individuals can touch the world in the same way as these basic yet powerful elements do; maybe not, but maybe so.

* * *

The steady rain that's been falling for most of the day is finally letting up. If you lift your nose to the air you can smell the spring flowers, the woodsy scent of cut trees, and the salty air as it rides in waves off of the sea. The gray sky has been delivering showers to the already soggy earth the entire day. Most children have been forced to remain inside playing board games, or watching T.V. They are waiting for the time when they can once again go outside and play until the fading light and the call of their parents will bring them back inside their homes.

A little boy with short-cropped, sandy-blond hair and large brown eyes winks at the family cat who curls herself around the child's leg. He giggles to himself. Last night he emerged victorious over one of the frequent, but good-spirited battles with his younger sister over which of them would get to take the pet to their room for the night.

Maybe he would let Linda win tonight, he considers with a mischievous smile. His thoughts are interrupted as the last distant rumble of thunder clamors like a bowling ball down the street. He pats his companion gently on the head and makes ready for his getaway in true cowboy fashion. The boy calls out a farewell to his mother; he'll be back in time for dinner. He gusts out the front door like a mini tornado.

His mother, Elfriede, knows better than to try and convince her son to stay indoors a moment longer. Scattered raindrops still sprinkle the pavement and rooftops, but Steve is a force unto himself. He is beckoning his friends to join him. Elfriede smiles, hearing his laughter take to the air like an untied balloon. She shakes her head, laughing herself now. She knows her boy all too well. Once again he forgot something. A small jacket rests on a hanger in a hallway closet. What would a force like the wind need with a jacket anyway?

1

Zero Hour

If you're lucky enough, maybe a few times in your life you will catch a glimpse of a shooting star as it blazes its way to earth. The beautiful sight of such speed and light is unforgettable. And if you're lucky enough, maybe once in your lifetime you will cross paths with someone who burns just as hot and bright as a shooting star; a person who is so unique that he will change the way you look at the world, and you are a better person for having the experience. I was indeed fortunate enough to have been influenced by such a special individual. His name was Steve Prefontaine.

I only ever got to exchange a few words with Steve over the fourteen years that I knew him. I can say I watched with great interest how he transitioned from an energetic, but sometimes uncertain, boy into a strong and determined man. Being witness to this transformation influenced the course of my own life; the shy, lonely bookworm of a kid found what it took to become a dedicated, world-traveled sportswriter. You see, Steve showed me what being a true athlete is about. It's not the money, fame, or victory dances. Being an athlete is a gift, but it's also a choice; a choice about the kind of person you are, how you treat others, and how you approach your sport. This much is true of every one of us; runner or writer, actor or architect, mill worker or musician. How you are is who you are. Steve taught me that too.

Steve once said "To give anything less than your best is to sacrifice the Gift." I carry those words with me every day of my life, especially when times get tough. Maybe once you know a little more about Steve or "Pre" as he became known to the world, he and his words will be an inspiration to you too.

My name is Owen and, as I said, I'm a writer - a storyteller - and I'd like to tell you a story.

* * *

My first memories of Steve Prefontaine begin during our years in grade school. We were classmates at Blossom Gulch School in Coos Bay, Oregon. I didn't talk much then, or hang out with other kids. I had my books, and studying was everything to me. It was my escape.

I felt a little out of place in a town where the buzz of saws hummed in your ears most hours of the day. The people of Coos Bay understood that survival meant a commitment to exhausting work and battling the harsh elements. Men like Steve's father worked outside where the relentless wind blew pelting rain from every direction. A child like Steve would put his hand into his father's and feel the thick calluses from the many hours of labor. These men didn't take "sick days". They just did what needed to be done to take care of their families.

I wasn't tough like the loggers or the fishermen. They were a bit like super-heroes to me - like the characters in one of my books. Heck, I didn't even have the grit of most boys on my block!

If you were a boy in Coos Bay you had to be a little rough cut. You had to prove that you could stand on your own and you didn't let your guard down. Some boys took that to the extreme and ended up getting into lots of trouble when they were older. They were never able to see past being all about the macho and what life had to offer.

There was one fierce little lad, a kid who could surely stand on his own but was also known to his friends as being real and honest. Steve Prefontaine spoke his mind, even at a young age. And the kid had guts too.

"Steve was someone you'd want on your side in a fight."

That's what one of his buddies said of him. Steve wasn't one to instigate a fight, but more likely to stand up for someone being unfairly treated. Later in life, his all out assault on behalf of those at the mercy of an unjust system would change the world of amateur sports for the better. His fierceness made a difference.

My house was not far from Steve's and the group he hung out with. Many days I would see them heading out to the "Indian Ledges"[1] (don't ask me where the name came from), a wooded hill area near the school. They would play for hours in the mud, building forts and imagining all kinds of exotic adventures. Their excited voices filled the air in contrast to the eerie stillness of the place. The ledges kept a secret

---

[1] some later generations of children called the place the Indian Legends

silence. It was removed from the constant song of the saws, and when there, you felt like you had left Coos Bay and stepped into another, more enchanted place. That didn't stop Steve and his pals, of course, from hooting and hollering whenever they felt the need!

Now that I'm all grown up I sometimes imagine an older, peaceful Steve walking through his old neighborhood and listening for the joyful voices of other children at play. It's one of the first impressions I have, like the briny air that welcomes me whenever I come home to Coos Bay.

The first time I saw Steve run was in a completely unofficial capacity. Games of tag were a constant in the neighborhood. Jay Farr got hold of his dad's mechanical stop watch and organized races. He did look the part of a meet organizer with his impressive timepiece. He even had a clip board to record each boy's progress as they raced in between the telephone poles.

Maybe that's where Steve's reverence of time, down to the nanosecond, began. To see Steve run later in life was to witness an unstoppable force in motion. His finely tuned body was an instrument connecting with the track, like a gifted musician laying his fingers on a piano. Steve's head cocked to one side, eyes brimming with resolve, focused on the seconds ticking away on the clock. He defied time with his speed.

In those early days a race, game of tag, or any other activity that involved good amounts of whooping and shouting, ceased as soon as Mrs. Farr rang her dinner bell. The boys would give each other slight jabs and playful shoves as a way of saying "See ya later", which, if the weather was good, meant after dinner.

Kirk Gamble lived in our neighborhood too. He had known Steve since the third grade. Their birthdays were only weeks apart, but the way they approached play was altogether different. Kirk said Steve had an intensity that no one could match and Kirk simply couldn't keep up with. Steve was a wild mustang that no one could throw a saddle over. Gradually, the shy, more reserved Kirk gravitated towards a group of kids who were a little more low-keyed in keeping with Kirk's nature. But it was always the same in the fall of each year.

"O.K. Race me!"

This was the high-spirited greeting Kirk received when he and Steve returned to school after summer vacation. Steve would jet up to Kirk and challenge him right in the middle of the school yard.

"I don't know where it came from, his need to race me like that. I could beat him till about the fifth grade, then I just turned him down. I knew he would win. All that fury wore me out!" Kirk reflected.

When Kirk signed up for cross country in his sophomore year, the memory of Steve's fury would inspire his childhood friend to set a few records of his own.

"I was a little afraid when I joined the team," Gamble explained years later. "You know, that Steve's fantastic energy would overwhelm me again. But that same unending capacity for activity that overtook me as a kid gave me the courage and the confidence to put everything I had into my sport during high school. When I was around Steve I wanted to give my best. Those were some of the most unforgettable years of my life."

Looking back as an adult, I too can see what I could not fully understand as a child; that Steve was unique from a very early age. He was a member of my Cub Scout pack, and his mom was a den mother. As fate would have it, our leader was a Mr. Walter McClure; a man who would come to share an unbreakable bond with Steve.

Mr. McClure, known as 'Mac' to those close to him, brought a bit of his father's military background to the troop. We were all expected to have our hair cut and combed, and our clothes neat and clean - ship shape! Steve never gave Mr. McClure any trouble; in fact I can remember Steve looking up at our leader with big brown eyes filled with interest and respect. His concentration was such that he was expecting Mr. McClure to weave a riotous and wonderful story at any moment and Steve didn't want to miss a minute of it.

Steve didn't want to miss a minute of anything. He could go from being the attentive and polite scout to a whirlwind of energy exploding into the woods with his kid sister Linda, Jay, Jim, John and the gang. Steve's street was enfolded by all the places he most treasured: the secretive Indian Ledges, his schools and the life-giving bay. That is to say, all roads in Coos Bay eventually led to the water. The Aquarian was right at home in any body of water; whether immersed in the bay, swimming the local rivers, or floating easefully on the wide, expansive ocean. Steve may have appeared to have wings on his feet when he ran, but he took to the water like Poseidon. Steve was ready for all kinds of action and he took advantage of it.

Young Prefontaine may not have been spectacular at everything he tried, but he did possess a natural athletic ability and a determination to try almost anything. When skateboards were the latest rage on the block, Steve and Linda made their own fashioned from the wheels they had removed from strap-on metal roller skates and attaching them to plywood cutout boards. I watched Steve as he pumped hard with one foot to gain the momentum to glide his way down Elrod. I saw his not so graceful attempts on the homemade board, which provided him with quite a challenge to stay balanced. Every time he faltered or fell off, he'd shrug and get back on again.

Even when the boards were taken and carefully hidden by their father who feared his children could get hurt, the crafty Steve and Linda had no trouble finding their master creations and rode during the day when dad was at work. The kids returned the skateboards to their father's hiding spot before he came home in the evening. Steve and Linda figured what their dad didn't know wouldn't hurt.

Steve's passion for adventure was something that could not be denied. It was like he regarded his body as the means by which he could experience all of life. Kind of like how we use our tongues to experience food, and our noses to take in all the different scents. Steve used his arms, legs, hands, feet; he threw his total self into activities, like diving into a pool in order to feel the exhilarating splash against his skin.

Up until I was ten-years old, I thought I was the only one who was different. I wasn't interested in sports or cars, the usual things most boys of Coos Bay were crazy about. Some of the other students would call me a "four-eyed freak". It didn't matter that I got good grades. I still wasn't one of the cool kids, much less one of the tough ones.

Then, one day, I noticed Steve at his desk. He was hunched over a piece of paper, a pencil gripped tightly in his left hand. He was working on an art project, sketching a house. The others had finished the assignment and were enjoying a bit of free time, milling around the classroom and trying to talk quietly as our teacher graded papers. Steve was still working.

I watched the way his lips moved silently while his pencil glided over the surface of the paper, as if he was an architect laboring over an original design. His teeth sank into his upper lip. He was completely focused on the task at hand. The little desk was a grand drawing board to Steve. The boy in perpetual motion was content to be right where he was. I hadn't had much experience of Steve like that.

Steve and his friend Jim Seyler were frequently banished to opposite corners of the classroom by our teacher for "too much goofing around." Even then, they'd steal glances at one another, causing the goofing to begin all over again. I got a kick out of their silliness. At least I really enjoyed watching someone dare to be so free.

Once, while walking home from school, I had seen Steve swinging out from a towering tree. He must have climbed up thirty feet or so and grabbed onto a branch and swung out, calling to Jim to join him. I couldn't believe my eyes! I felt scared just watching him from a distance, but when he landed like a paratrooper on the ground below, he didn't show any signs of distress. He simply rolled over, stood up, and brushed himself off. The grin on his face was as big as the Cheshire Cat's. Lots of things about Steve were contagious, like his smile.

Steve wasn't smiling as he kept at his drawing that particular day. The noise level in the classroom was rising, but he remained absorbed in his art.

"Hey Steve!" one of the boys called out to him, but Steve didn't raise his head. "Ya think you're gonna finish that by the end of the year?"

The boy continued in the usual way classmates like to josh with one another. The girls giggled.

"Guys," Another boy turned to the class who had formed a small circle near Steve's desk. "Don't bother a master at work!"

"Check it out!" Jim pointed to the picture. The house looked like something out of a magazine, it was so detailed. "That's pretty darn good."

The rest of the kids looked on impressed by Steve's work, but still attempting to distract him. No one could be so steady, could they? Steve looked up from his picture just long enough to rest his fiery eyes on each of their faces. Our teacher directed everyone to take their seats. She suggested that Steve put the assignment aside for the time being. He didn't offer any disrespect. He just turned his eyes back to his work and said "I'd like to finish what I started, please."

I knew then I wasn't the only one who was different by having a great interest for something. But I also knew, for the first time in my life that being different wasn't such a bad thing.

I was never in the company of Steve's family, but I heard that they were pretty close. I was an only child, and I wondered what it must have been like for Steve being the only boy in the family. He was a big brother to his sister Linda, and a little brother to sister Neta. Ray, Steve's dad, was a carpenter. He built the family home, complete with a fence of his own design. Sometimes Mr. Prefontaine's special creation was painted blue, sometimes pink. One thing's for sure - it wasn't your average white picket fence. Steve's mother, Elfriede, was a seamstress. Ray met Elfriede in Germany during his time in the U.S. Army. Steve's German grandmother lived with the family too. Steve's first words were most likely German. It took him a while to distinguish between the two languages spoken in and outside his home. It's funny how Steve began his life with German words being so familiar to him. I bet no one could have guessed then that "Big Pre" would use that language knowledge years later as an Olympic competitor in Munich, Germany.

I still laugh when I think of the stories that were told to me about Steve as a young boy. Steve could be a devilish prankster. Together with Linda, the two were like lightning bolts striking at their activities with the highest of energy. The front room of the Prefontaine home was often used for spontaneous wrestling matches and general rough-housing. Everyone got involved too, even Mrs. Prefontaine. Jay Farr told me Steve's mom would do splits and back-bends for her young audience.

Steve also learned impeccable table manners from his mother who would prepare a huge breakfast every day. If you happened to be at the Prefontaine's for a sleep-over, and you weren't awakened the next morning by the commotion of Steve up and chasing after Linda, then the glorious smells from the kitchen would have your mouth watering. Mrs. Prefontaine made pancakes, various breakfast meats, and eggs. No one ever just got a bowel of cereal or toast offered to them. The Prefontaines were also very neatly dressed, with clean clothes and clean faces (unless they were outside!); and the home was spotless.

I overheard Jim Seyler talking to some boys in our class during recess one day in January. We had to be in fifth or sixth grade at the time. I was sitting on the steps close by, reading a book, as Jim was telling the guys about a birthday party he had recently attended for Steve. My ears pitched up like a rabbit in the woods when I heard Steve's name mentioned. I kept my book in front of me pretending to be engrossed in the pages so as not to appear to be eavesdropping, which I was!

The party was at the Prefontaine home; Steve, his family and three other boys. As usual, it was a formal yet warm gathering. The table was set with fine china, silverware and a beautifully embroidered white table cloth. Jim supposed it was from Mrs. Prefontaine's family in Germany. Whenever she had company, Steve's mom would make sure to put out the best for her guests. Her son's birthday party was no exception.

"Well," Jim was saying "Steve's mother was pouring red Kool Aid for each of us in these really fancy glasses. She asked us to be careful not to spill it, or get cake crumbs on the table, ya know - not to be slobs. But, within a few seconds of her pouring, I accidentally knocked over my full glass!"

I peaked over the top of my book. The distressed look on Jim's face even as he relived the moment was enough to convey how upset he must have been.

"There was dead silence at the table," Jim said grimly. His audience fell silent as well, imagining if they had been the perpetrators of such an infraction. After a brief pause Jim continued.

"Steve's mother cleared the table. I'm sure the tablecloth was ruined. And then she spread another cloth and reset the table. We were barely breathing. Man! I felt so bad!"

"And of course a couple of the guys had to go and make comments like 'Way to go Sy!' I know they were joshing, but come on! I just ruined Mrs. Pre's best tablecloth!"

"What did she do, Sy? Did she yell at ya?" one of the boys asked.

"No," Jim said. "I mean, I'm sure she was ticked, but she didn't say anything."

"What about Steve? Did he give it to ya?" the next question came with a laugh.

The young Seyler looked at each of his classmates as if deciding whether he should continue.

"Well... What did Steve do?" The boys pressed.

Jim caught the eyes of each of his listeners as he concluded in a quiet voice.

"The thing is, Steve, he just looked at me. And I knew that he knew exactly how I felt. He said it was an accident and I shouldn't feel bad about it. He was cool." Jim shrugged. "It was *his* birthday, but he cared about how *I* felt, ya know?"

"Yeah, that is kinda cool," the boys agreed shaking their heads.

The bell rang and the little cluster of young men broke apart – each reluctantly heading back towards the school building. I stayed on the step a moment longer, still pretending to be caught up in my book; but really I was thinking, "Yeah, that is very cool."

Although it was a strict household with certain rules to be obeyed, there was also permission for fun. From what I hear, there was a lot of love in that house. And love is what inspires any great and lasting accomplishment.

A kid in Coos Bay in the early 1960s didn't have many choices as to how to spend free time. Trouble was always waiting around the corner in the form of a tough gang. Sometimes trouble found Steve, and sometimes he found it. Steve wasn't one to back down from his beliefs. He spoke his mind for sure; but when push came to shove, he avoided raising a hand to strike another person. His quick wit, sharp tongue, and full throttle passion were his weapons, or peace-makers depending on how you look at it.

Jim and Steve stuck together to keep away from the gangs that would no doubt lead them down the wrong path. The two boys spent lots of time with their HO cars and tracks. These mini models of some of the boy's favorite cars - Chevy's, Fords, and race cars - kept them busy for hours. When they weren't talking about cars, they were talking about the girls they liked, and there were plenty of girls they liked! Saturday afternoons were special because the boys could go to the movie house and catch an afternoon show while munching on popcorn and candy.

The distance to the theatre was about a mile. If they weren't riding their bikes, Jim and Steve (and whoever else happened to tag along) ran the whole way. When you were with Steve, running was part of the relationship – and it was always a race. Jim was more of a sprinter and could outrun Steve in the shorter distances, but he would soon fade to the amazing endurance of his friend. Falling behind, Jim would eventually meet Steve at the movie where he would be waiting with a grin from ear to ear as if to say "I won again." There was no mean-spiritedness in this, just the boundless energy of a boy who may not have even realized then how talented he was.

Our grade school years passed in the wink of an eye. I spent most of my summers in the library, and Steve spent his frolicking at the pool in Mingus Park where he would later work as a lifeguard in his high school years. Life in Oregon, as in most places, is never perfect. Making the transition from grammar school to high school is a major change. I chose to play it safe and stick to what I knew best. But Steve, who had visions of joining the Marshfield High football team, was handed yet another challenge, another tall tree to jump from; and jump he did.

Eighth grade; I was tall and gangly and Steve was about five feet, maybe 100 pounds if that. It was a time in my life when I decided that I would try to fit in a little more with my classmates. I knew of no better way to accomplish that goal than to attend some of the junior high football games.

Football and football players receive an automatic, unchallenged respect. I knew a little bit about the game; not much, but enough to understand why someone of Steve's height and weight spent most of his time sitting on the bench. I could tell early on that Steve had all the spirit and then some for the sport. I was merely getting up the courage to *go* to the games, but Steve was doing his best to be *in* them.

And then it happened. I can't say I recall for sure the exact date and time as if it were some extraordinary event like an eclipse or a meteor shower, but it was indeed a very significant happening. Track and field in the US, particularly in Oregon, was beginning to command a respect all its own. Steve and I were in the same physical education class. The principal decided to make long distance running a part of the program. As usual, I wasn't up for anything that involved a lot of sweating. The burning I got in my lungs was enough to make me slow down to a wobbly walk.

But Steve just shined it on. It seemed the longer he had to run, the faster he moved, quickly cutting the distance between himself and the leaders. I exchanged curious glances with a fellow classmate. Freed from his desk and the demands of others, Steve's running was fueled by strength of mind as much as by strength of body. Steve had found his sport.

I don't mean to sound preachy when I talk about the lessons that I learned from Steve. I share them with you in the hope that you will see a part of yourself in him like I did; and learn from him, like I and so many others did.

You may have noticed that even if you are good at something, that doesn't give you a free pass to slack off and simply expect success. However talented we are, we still have to work at it. At times it can seem like an uphill battle, even though our efforts may appear to be the most natural thing in the world.

2

Pre Flight

When Steve discovered he could run, he was fired up about it. If Steve was fired up about something, it was like a spark to a powder keg. In the spring of 1965, when Steve was still in junior high, he spotted some of the older boys - track team members - running intervals. The way one of the team members recalls it:

"And along comes this punky little eighth grader saying he could keep up with us. 'Course, we knew better, so we encouraged him to take a turn at it. Why not teach the little kid a lesson? Well, after the first two sets the kid says 'It's not so bad.' He was starting to break a good sweat, so we let him continue. After the third and fourth sets he started to slow down a little. We asked him what was wrong, ya know, laughing 'cos we knew he was tired out. But, I gotta say, that kid didn't turn tail and go home; he just took some deep breaths and said 'Gimmie a minute and I'll catch up with you.'"

This might very well have been a defining moment in Steve's development as a runner. The challenge these older, more experienced boys put to him - and the way he took it on - might have confirmed for him what he was made of and given him a preview of how much effort goes into being the best.

You might think I was jealous of Steve. After all, in his freshman year he went from seventh man on the track team to second. But he earned each one of his victories. It was as if the times that he did lose, he would become that much more determined to better himself for the next time.

Steve had ample opportunities to improve. I'm certain there will never be another who will be able to duplicate that special mix of fire, guts and determination. People watched in awe as the months and years went by. Steve continued to ratchet up his workouts and his goals as a runner and a person.

One night at the supper table my father was telling my mother and me how Steve had become one of the "morning regulars." My dad delivered bread for a local company, which meant he was up and working very early in the morning.

"That Prefontaine, he's a little powerhouse," my father laughed. "Ya know, the police used to wonder what the heck the kid would be doing out running the streets at all hours; and now, well, we just know to expect him. Thing I don't get is, I *have* to be out there that early, but he *chooses* to be. That boy probably works as hard as any man I know. He gives me a wave as he passes by."

My father nodded his head in approval and ploughed his fork into his mashed potatoes. He was rarely impressed by the actions of people my age, but Steve most definitely endeared himself to my dad that year.

It wasn't only my father who spied Steve on his daily runs; I did too. I took a job delivering groceries, planning ahead for my college tuition. I would see Steve running everywhere; on the dunes, along the rain-swept streets, between the telephone poles. As he whipped by with the wind - his hair blown back, arms and legs pumping uphill like a miniature locomotive - I pictured him as Mercury with his winged shoes flying down the streets of Coos Bay with a singular purpose.

It was because of Steve that I found my purpose. When I was a freshman, my English composition teacher suggested I try my hand at writing for the school newspaper - *The Ma-Hi Times*. I liked the idea. As fate would have it, the newspaper was in need of a staff writer to cover the school's sporting events. The editor was doubtful that a "nerdy book-type" like me would be the best person for such an assignment, but I impressed him with my knowledge of the basics and also with my writing. I got the job. Steve Prefontaine would be the ink for my paper. He sure did give me a lot to write about.

Steve's first year on the track team was a bit shaky, like a new colt finding his footing on solid ground. But he had the good fortune of having two coaches and several teammates who saw the talent waiting to be unleashed. Walter McClure (remember the Cub Scout leader?) who had been a great runner himself recognized the unpolished gem that would soon shine to the world as Pre. Phil Pursian, the assistant coach, was "the new kid on the block", and someone Pre and the other team members would occasionally go to in times of frustration. A lot of people made the sad mistake of seeing the terrific amount of confidence and drive packed into the five feet plus of a young boy and wrote it off as cockiness or arrogance.

But I know that people, like stories and words, are never that simple. That "plus" *was* Steve - Pre, someone who very early on decided that he was flat out going to be the best, no matter what anyone else thought.

Pre could not only inspire, but be inspired as well. He looked up to and respected his coaches for their experience and dedication to the team. The coaches made sure everyone understood that this was indeed a team, and each member was there to support the others. They were like a small army and their battle ground was the track. During his early days running for Marshfield, Pre became friends with a few of the older guys - guys who had been running and setting school records for a few seasons already. Along comes Pre and he begins to break those records in short order. Some kept their distance from him, not wanting anything to do with the brash little freshman, and some saw an opportunity to teach and learn.

Tom Huggins was one year older than Pre, but the two became fast friends. They lived on neighboring streets and developed a routine - running together every day, twice a day, even on the weekends. No matter what the weather, they would run. They would take turns coasting to the other's house to start the day.

"There were some days - especially the stormy ones - that I'd have to knock on Pre's window to wake him up. He'd do the same for me."

I remember interviewing Tom for my *Get to Know the Track and Field Team* article series. Tom was one of those Marshfield record setters, someone who Coach McClure spoke highly of. I suspect that he was somebody young Pre looked up to as well.

"Can you tell me about what it's like running with the other guys on the team?" I asked Tom.

"You mean, Pre?" Tom smiled knowing that lots of people were starting to take notice of the new kid with star potential.

"Well, yeah, what's it like running with Steve?"

"O.K. First of all, none of us call him 'Steve.' That is, unless we're mad at him." Tom laughed.

"And do you get mad at him a lot?"

"Not usually. See, Pre has a confidence for sure. But he also has the drive. Not a lot of people understand what it takes to be a distance runner. It's a lot of time and pain and perseverance. Sure there are days when none of us wants to run, but that's where we help each other. We rely on each other. When you run with a guy over ten miles a day, like I do with Pre, you get to know that guy pretty well."

"Some people are saying Steve..." I corrected myself. "...Pre is too confident - cocky even. Is that true?"

Tom shook his head. "People who say he's cocky don't really know him."

"How so?"

"Because if Pre is your friend, then you know that you have someone who would seriously lay down his life for you. He's that loyal. Maybe he has a big mouth, but his heart Is just as big. Hey, ya gotta understand," Tom continued. "You know how popular football is."

I nodded. I knew all too well whenever a player passed me in the hallway at school, I instantly felt invisible.

"Pre and me, we wanted to play on the team; but we were both too small. So we found what we were good at in running. This track team we have, it's good; the guys are talented. And Pre works really hard. Every guy on the team knows it too. I'm not so sure a football player could keep up with him."

"Or you!" I added.

Tom grinned. "We are a pretty tough lot, us runners."

I agreed.

I interviewed Kirk Gamble (the same Kirk Gamble who had been worn out as a kid by Steve's tireless play) for my story as well. He was sipping a soda in the cafeteria during lunch period.

"Pre can just about never do an *easy* run, even during practice." Kirk took a bite of a Mars bar. "He goes at it with all he has. Case in point:" Kirk put down his candy bar. "We all do morning runs, pairing up with someone else from the team. I wouldn't want to do a morning run with Pre." Kirk laughed at his confession. "He pours it on, at 6am no less!" Kirk gave me a "can you believe it?" look and continued. "Pre does about six miles in the morning and at night, and that's along with school, homework and track practice!"

Kirk wasn't too shabby a runner himself. He'd been a distance runner since middle school. He and Pre participated in the high school track and cross country programs at Marshfield, and the "unofficial" winter program. I use the term "unofficial" because during the winter months it was close to impossible to run outside. Few to no schools then had indoor track facilities. There were approximately two meets in the winter and nothing else for a runner to look forward to until the spring.

Marshfield did have a very nice gymnasium, however, which the track team made use of during the months of harsh weather. The gym consisted of three floors where the boys could run laps on the upper level. Twenty laps equaled one mile. The corners were very sharp. Running at full speed to take one of these difficult turns would break a runner's stride considerably. Imagine Pre going full tilt and having to slow up so as not to crash into a wall, or fall down a stairwell! Speaking of stairs, they too were used as part of the workouts, each member of the team running up and down in repetition. These unusual workouts were an example of the dedication of the Marshfield runners and the creativity of the coaches. They wouldn't allow a thing like nasty weather to impede their training.

One of the winter meets was held at Reedsport High School about an hour away from Coos Bay. Doors were opened and the hallways of the school were transformed into an indoor track. One lap around the halls was a quarter mile. Steve passed everyone, again and again. The corners weren't so tough here, because of some built-in banked turns. The runners could more easily glide through the double doors on their way around.

When Steve was a sophomore he placed fifth in the Oregon Invitational, a meet that brought in the best runners from the entire state. Then came the outdoor season which didn't go as well as Steve had hoped. Here's a bit from a story I wrote for the school paper after one of those events.

Steve Prefontaine, a fresh breath of life that has blown onto the Marshfield High track scene, is going to be somebody to watch, no doubt. He has great energy, push and promise. He may need to harness some of that energy, as today I spotted Steve racing down the track, not in his own event but during the events of fellow team members. He was lending his enthusiastic support. It seemed as if he wanted to share some of his spunk with the others...

It was a sight to behold. Picture this little fireball suited up in his school colors. He was like a flash of purple lightning darting down the sidelines, his mop top hair sweaty and sticking to his forehead, his cheeks red with exertion and his feet keeping an even pace with the competitors. All the while he was shouting out encouragement and advice in a hoarse but confident voice.

My story on that particular event ended like this:

...Pre finished third in his own event. A lesson was learned this sunny, warm afternoon. Coach believes Pre tuckered himself out by cheering on his teammates. That could very well be and, judging by the resolute look on Pre's face, he won't soon be taking third place again.

He didn't stop providing support to his fellow runners, though. Pre set the bar higher for everyone who ran with him. His teammates had tremendous respect for him because he pulled them along, daring them to go faster and farther with him. He was a jackrabbit on the track with everyone chasing his tail.

Coach McClure recalls that Pre made good use of every minute of his workouts.

"He wasn't the last to leave the gym. He'd be one of the first, because he knew what he had to get done and he'd just be about getting to it."

You can bet the others took notice. Even in his greatest, record setting victories, Pre always would take a moment to encourage another - share the spotlight with an athlete who may have been defeated in the race, but achieved a personal best. Much has been made about Steve's fire, but it was tempered with grace.

Fran Worthen was a young girl whose house was situated on one of Pre's running routes. Like me, she caught her first glimpse of Pre powering down the streets of Coos Bay. That was her only introduction to someone of whom she would later claim "His friendship meant everything to me." It's easy to see why. When Fran was a freshman at Marshfield, boy's and girl's track were separate. The girls didn't get a lot of support for their athletic efforts. This was before Title 9. Female athletes, no matter how much potential they showed in high school, could not look forward to receiving any athletic scholarships for college. Fran was a member of the GAA (Girl's Athletic Association) which provided assistance and support at the boy's track meets.

Pre took the time to encourage Fran. He helped to foster her belief in herself and her abilities as a sprinter. "He was my champion," Fran said of her much-loved friend. Pre would continue to have an impact on Fran's life.

During my teenage years my avid reading gave me the idea to try a few new activities. I thought I might excel at something. But usually, if things got too tough, I got going the other way - onto something else. I didn't like failure, nobody does.

Running is a tough sport. The longer the distance you go, the effort you make to shorten your time and increase your speed makes for great pain. Your lungs burn, your legs feel like logs, and your brain sends messages like: "Are you crazy? Stop this right now!"

The naïve kid I was would have understood if Steve had decided to try something else after his early defeats. I didn't know as much about Steve back then as I thought. It's a joke to me now when I consider the idea that maybe Steve would have given up. Quitting and Pre just didn't go together; and anyone who got to know Pre, even a little bit, knew that much.

Coach McClure said it was in those early losses that Pre began to find himself. He had the amazing ability to outrun the mental and physical pain of his sport. Coach had seen a lot of good runners come and go, and he was always a little wary of freshmen who showed great promise. Oftentimes, that hot spark in an athlete would burn out quickly. The following years usually brought disappointment and unfulfilled potential. Coach would invent special things to keep his runners motivated. He awarded T-shirts to those who racked up a certain number of miles throughout the months, and even years, on the team. Someone might be sporting a "300 Mile Club" T-shirt after a season. That was a decent accomplishment, but Pre's T-shirt read "2000 Mile Club"!

Freshman year. Pre went from the middle of the pack to number two man, and he also lettered in cross country. He soon did away with any doubts coach may have had about his ability to sustain the pace. Pre had a depth that his coaches had not seen in any other runner before. He could also be a bit headstrong, and that's when Coach Pursian would provide a calming resource. A little bit of wisdom and guidance went a long way with Pre. He took what people said - especially those he respected - to heart.

Pre returned to cross country in the fall of his junior year, announcing to his coaches that he would go undefeated. Both McClure and Pursian thought that Pre had no idea of what he was getting himself into. He didn't appreciate who his competitors were and how difficult it would be to beat them.

"But we didn't share our doubts with Pre," coach Pursian remembers. "We just told him that was certainly a good goal to have. We wanted to encourage him."

Within a week and a half into the season, the coaches realized this was a different kid out on the field. This kid had a definite fire in his eyes. It wasn't just words for Pre when he said "I want to be the best." He knew that meant not just challenging the other runners but, even more so, himself.

Pre made little signs of his goals and posted them in his room. He'd write things like "State Champ", "Remember Last Year?", "4.08 or better." And usually he'd have a special message about the person he intended to defeat that year - "Beat Crooks", for instance. Doug Crooks was in the same grade as Pre and was the best freshman miler in the state.

I even heard that in the beginning of his training, Pre's mom wasn't too sure about her son doing all that running. She felt that schoolwork and chores were more important. And so she would sneak into Pre's room and shut off his alarm clock which he had set for 5:30 each morning. Elfriede felt her son needed his rest. That's a mom for ya! Pre respected her enough to make sure his chores and homework were done before he took on anything else. It was a sign of their unspoken agreement and mutual respect for one another.

In fact, Steve had such love and respect for his parents and his diverse heritage that he participated in German folk dancing lessons. The hall where the classes were held was so ancient that many Coos Bay residents still accessed it by boat. Steve's stride was one of confidence (dressed in full alpine costume!) as he met friend John Knutson who had come to give him a ride home one day. John was a bit taken aback, seeing a side of Steve he had not been privy to before. But knowing Steve as he did, John simply smiled and delivered his dancing friend to the Prefontaine abode.

Make no mistake – those who ran with Pre (and knew him as a child as John did) understood exactly what the guy was made of. John recounted for me a time when he and another track team member, Roger Bingham, were on a run with Pre. It was a sticky hot day, and the boys were running uphill. The dirt road was riddled with sizeable furrows and the dust they kicked up stuck to their perspiring, fatigued bodies. Pre had already made it back to the coach's van, while John and Roger were still trying to negotiate their way up the hill.

"Pre sprints back and meets us mid-way to try and coax us on," John describes the experience. "Roger and I were just trying to breathe and Pre is running backwards, dodging the ruts in the road and chatting away to us the whole time. We couldn't respond even if we wanted to. We were too winded."

By his senior year, Pre was doing his morning runs alone. No one could keep up with the exhausting tests he set for himself during those early hours. Even his coaches didn't know what he was up to. He would start his run hard and continue full on until he had nothing more to give. Then he would look around for a landmark - a street sign or house number - so that the next day he would go out same as before, only this time push himself further than the previous day. He would do this day after day, until he got within a half mile of his house. Only then did he slow down.

"That's got to be Pre." A phrase I will never forget. It sums up the feeling a person had when seeing Steve run for the first time. The person to coin that phrase was the man who would be one of Pre's coaches at the University Of Oregon.

Pre was focused on winning the state title as a high school junior when Coach Bill Dellinger first saw Steve run. Coach recalls that he was looking through his binoculars at the boys filling the start line about a half-mile away. He noticed a particular young man, most especially the fierceness of his eyes.

"The intensity in his face as the gun went off; I thought that's got to be Pre."

When hearing Coach Dellinger's words, all I could think of was that little boy in the fifth grade staring down anyone who may have criticized him for not being like the rest. He never looked away, but right at their eyes as if to say "So what if I'm not like you? I'm not afraid to be who I am." Pre's fearlessness and perseverance paid off. He kept up quite a pace, and no one could get too close to him. He made good on his word of going undefeated, and winning the state title in his junior year. At seventeen Pre set an all-time Oregon two-mile best, running at 9:01.3.

Pre was resourceful too. His energy wasn't just focused on running. He held down several part time jobs during high school. He helped his dad with the clean-up on carpentry jobs and worked at a gas station. If that weren't enough, I remember when Pre and a friend decided they were going to paint cars to earn money. They didn't have any experience -except that most boys in Coos Bay (except yours truly) knew a good deal about cars. They did a pretty good job of it too; at least, I don't think anyone with a freshly painted car that summer asked for their money back!

In many ways Steve was like every other high school kid. He had a girlfriend, Elaine, and they spent time together when they could - nothing extravagant. You have to keep in mind in those days we didn't have cell phones, e-mail or huge theme parks and shopping malls to go and spend an entire day in - not to mention a small fortune. At night Steve, Elaine and most all the other kids their age would go out "dragging the gut" as it was termed. Now I know you can't possibly guess what that was about! Well, picture this; all the guys would polish up their cars, make sure their "wheels" were shiny and clean so they could cruise down the familiar drag of road between the Arctic Circle and the A&W. They drove slowly. This was one time Steve didn't race. He and the others wanted to be seen by everyone else out and about.

Steve wasn't so cool to be above being a gentleman though. One night, when an unexpected rainstorm blew in just as he and Elaine were heading into the movies, I saw him charge around to her side of the car to open her door and escort her under his umbrella into the theatre. That was pretty suave.

Steve and Elaine would go to school games and the beach. Sometimes they took Steve's sister Linda along with them. They shared many of the same experiences as any pair of high school sweethearts from a small town - like going to the senior prom together.

Marshfield High's track team is known as The Pirates. A pirate is a thief who rollicks on the high seas. I've thought about Pre, this Aquarius water carrier, as a pirate; but not the usual kind with a black patch over one eye, smoking a pipe, sporting a parrot on his shoulder and shouting "Ahoy mates!"

The only thing Pre stole was the hearts of the fans that began to fill Pirate Stadium. They came to cheer on this young man who they had seen running all over town, as he cut out record times on the track, pushing himself to go faster and farther. Pre was more than a pirate; he was an explorer.

Imagine the great sailors and astronomers, like Magellan and Galileo. Most of their contemporaries were fearful of what terrors might lay beyond the limits of their narrow world view. But these two great men, and others like them, preferred to seek and embrace the progress that would come from searching beyond the known boundaries. Pre wanted to travel to the outer limits of his sport, and then go further. He was a one-man ship, charting the seas and stars of his own abilities. Pre could make a self-assured statement such as "What I want to be is number one", and people paid attention. This was partly because Pre's eyes held the truth and fire of his feelings, and partly because his genuine smile was a sure sign that he was unique, more than just a kid bragging about as-yet unattained victories.

Pirates seek to fill their ships with stolen treasure. At the end of the day it's all about how much they have attained - how much they have taken from others. The treasure Pre sought was not so much winning in order to snatch victory from his rivals, although he did enjoy a good competition, no doubt. His prize was the knowledge that he had done his very best, challenged his toughest opponent - himself. He paid close attention to those other boys straining and reaching as they ran so close together. But when Pre broke from the pack, his eyes were focused on the clock - his time. The huffs of his competitors were drowned out by the pounding of his heartbeat and the movement of his legs and feet, one in front of the other, faster yet. He shouted to himself first and foremost "Go Pre!"

Pre was a most unusual pirate, because he was a generous mate. He gave a stunning show to the ever increasing crowds who turned out to see him. As he matured, he also gave of himself to those less fortunate, and the people most had forgotten about.

I believe that 1969 at Marshfield was the beginning of the unbreakable bond between the people of Oregon ("Pre's people") and Steve Prefontaine. He would later say after winning the 1971 AAU National Championship, "These Oregon people are the best in the world. I could do anything here I think. With people like this, how can you lose?"

Pre didn't lose much his last year in high school. He stepped up his game, faithfully training under the guidance of Coaches

McClure and Pursian. They worked together in order for Pre to improve his time and his form.

Excerpt from Marshfield High News Paper:

April 25, 1969

Steve Prefontaine Sets New Record

The calendar says spring, but there is a definite nip in the air. The Corvallis Invitational is a night meet. It feels a little strange to be waiting for a race to begin at 9 pm. As I reach for my jacket the runners begin to take their places at the starting line. I can clearly see Steve Prefontaine's head of blonde hair bobbing among the other hopefuls. Pre is representing Marshfield in his final year as a high school student. He is shaking out his arms and legs, like he's just jumped out of the shower and is trying to quickly dry off.

I would have never supposed he might feel a legion of butterflies in his stomach as he later told Coach McClure. To us spectators, Pre seems very sure of himself. I have a suspicion that he is aiming to set a new record, and frankly, as I wait with the anxious and enthusiastic folks on these cold bleachers, I can feel my stomach turn slightly. I want this for Pre, heck we all do! He's got us under his spell.

And they're off! In a matter of seconds the runners move from the start position to their all-out attack on the cinder track. Pre's first lap is a bit slow. My heart does a flip flop, but my head tells me he is far from beat. Sure enough, his pace steadily increases with each lap and, on the last one, Pre is out in front. The race is his and he kicks it out, finishing the two mile at 8:41.5. Our fearless pirate has taken the old record of 8:48.4 and claimed it for his own.

Do you know what I realized as I waited for that race to begin? There we were, the crowd of supporters assuming Pre's confident stride meant he never felt a moment of self-doubt. This incorrect assumption on the part of others only increased as Pre matured as a person and an athlete. That's the funny thing about excellence. When most of us see it in another, we automatically believe the person to be full of confidence - full of himself. We don't realize that this person is the same as us; and he feels the same pains and fears that we all do. The night of Pre's Corvallis victory I was beginning to really understand that, right before my eyes, was being unveiled in Pre what it takes to be a true champion; and it isn't swagger or boasts, but a wholehearted effort to backbreaking work and the complete love of one's sport. Pre understood that, and despite his fear and pain he said, in essence, "Bring it on!"

Steve also won the mile and two mile events at both the district and state meets that year. He gave up the chance at setting additional personal records so that Marshfield could win as a team. If he would have tried for more, he would have had nothing left to give for the team. He made that choice and was content with accomplishing wins in both races at both meets. No one in Oregon had done that before.

Pre took his leave of Marshfield and Coos Bay in style. During one meet he ran the mile in under 4:10. It was one of the most exciting races I ever witnessed. Pre held the lead for most of the race, but then one ambitious competitor surged by him. Pre immediately picked up the pace and reclaimed the lead. Once again his challenger hung close and passed for a second time. These were the only two with a shot for the win. Pre called up his reserves and went out ahead. But his competitor was soon on his heals surging for a third time to take the lead.

There is one word that has been used over and over again by friends, fellow athletes, and sports enthusiasts to describe Pre – "*fierce!*"

Pre was nothing less than fierce in that race. He simply refused to be beat; by the challenger, by the clock, and most especially by himself. He dug down deep, took the lead and held it for the win.

After having the exhausting experience of running two events that meet, Pre came up to his good friend Jay Farr and fellow teammates getting set to run the mile relay. Everyone on the team was as important to Pre as his own accomplishments. He was still trying to catch his breath, and his sweats were draped over his shoulder. "It's all up to you guys now," he urged his fellow pirates on for the team win.

I spoke with Coach Pursian after the meet to get his impressions. He gave me a glimpse into some of the unmatched power of the team.

"Pre has a vision, and all the other track team members buy into his vision. Each boy is doing things, each in his own way that he didn't think he could. That's because of Pre."

Pre was also the kind of person who believed in encouraging kids. I believe that kids have the freshest and most open-minded view of the world. They see the wonder of it all; they are curious and ask lots of questions. That's how Pre was too. He was such a natural with the younger crowd - "a pied piper", his friends said. His dedication to helping kids started early in his life and continued all the way through till the end.

As high school seniors, Pre and his buddy Jay Farr visited local grade schools to talk to students about the dangers of smoking. They brought a smoking machine with them to demonstrate the damage cigarettes did to the body. Even in college and after, when he was so well known and his time in such demand, Pre would continue to devote a good chunk of his time to work with kids one-on-one to encourage their pursuit of excellence, and always to keep them asking "Why?"

Steve had a way (and still does) of bringing people together. I think of the constellations. When I first learned to look for Orion, the Big Dipper or Cygnus, I couldn't find a pattern among what seemed like a random cluster of stars. But when I took a moment to step back and really focus, I could see the formation of "The Hunter", his stars aligning to create a beautiful design. It was a different kind of stargazing on May 9, 1969 when one little star brought together many.

Mark Paczesniak really liked baseball. He also liked music. Mark played in the school band with Steve through junior high, Steve on the cornet and Mark on the clarinet. Marshfield's baseball team had the benefit of Mark's athletic talent. Home games were held at Mingus Park, about a mile away from the stadium where the track team ran its meets. It just so happened, that one particular baseball game was set for the very same day on which Steve had made the public prediction that he was going to attempt to run a sub four minute mile at the Coos County Meet.

The athletics stadium was packed. It seemed like the whole population of Coos Bay had come out for the event. A representative from Sports Illustrated Magazine was in attendance as well.

A freshman by the name of Stan Goodell from the town of Bandon, Oregon was going for a record of his own that same race. He was trying to break a five minute mile. Nervous as he was, Stan was inspired by the slightly older Pre who was set to run only two lanes apart from the freshman.

Stan was well aware of Steve Prefontaine and his capabilities on the track. Since junior high, Stan had followed with great interest Pre's incredible progress. Stan knew how hard Pre worked; and on that wind-blown, chilly day in May, the presence of Pre gave Stan the courage to reach for his own goal. It would be that way for the rest of Stan's life. Kirk Gamble, a senior like Pre, was set to run the two mile.

Meanwhile, all those baseball folks at Mingus Park were "Pre-occupied." Mark and his Marshfield pirates obviously wanted to claim victory in their game, but at the same time they wanted to be at the track to cheer on their friend as he attempted his gutsy goal.

After six innings (baseball games then were only played for seven innings) the score was locked in a tie. Everyone consulted their watches and calculated. Pre would soon be running.

Both coaches came onto the field to talk with the umpire. The feelings of the players on both teams and the assembled crowd were united. Without much debate, it was decided that a seventh inning was not necessary. The game would be called a tie. The general consensus was that it was more important for that fireball of a runner to have the well earned support of all gathered there.

These were the people who had seen Steve tirelessly running through the streets of their town, and pumping gas into their cars where he worked. They had heard his laughter when he'd been falling about with the rest of the Coos Bay kids. These were the people who first knew that Steve was something unique, because he had found his gift and never once took it for granted. He was thankful for the opportunity, pushing himself to keep improving day after day. He was the example of perseverance and he deserved their encouragement.

The game was called and everybody boarded busses heading out to the track. They made it in time to see Pre run. He came in a little over four minutes (4:06.9 to be exact) - still winning the race - and not one spectator was disappointed. They saw Pre's great effort, his gratitude, and his spunk. They also knew that Steve Prefontaine was well on his way to making history. He had already made them proud.

Kirk Gamble clipped two seconds off his personal best in the two mile and set a county record that has stood unchallenged for decades.

"That was a very inspirational night for a lot of people," Kirk remembers. "There was something exceptional about the combination of Pre and Coach McClure; Pre was the motivation for the whole team and coach was the perfect teacher. Together, they made us all give more."

Kirk did learn from Steve. If you watch the footage of that race, as I have several times, you will see a young Kirk Gamble sprinting around the field encouraging Steve while he ran.

And Stan Goodell? Well, he ran 4:58, breaking a five minute mile. He still talks about that meet. He will never forget how Pre gave him something to strive for. Stan says that running is etched in his life forever. Each time he runs, he has a vision that urges him forward; he's racing against Pre in an effort to pass him. Even in his fantasy, Stan is aware he won't be able to do it, but it doesn't matter. In his mind's eye, Pre's fire is the spark that gives Stan the kick to his finish. That kick might not have happened were it not for the imaginings of one young man motivated by the great tenacity of another. I imagine that Pre would have given Stan a pat on the back and a generous smile for his valiant effort; something Pre would have understood better than anyone.

Stan has been coaching track for over thirty years and Pre is still the example for his young runners.

"It didn't matter who Pre was running against," Stan tells his students. "He was able to go beyond the limits. He gave 110% all the time, and that made us all want to be better."

Pre's positive impact wasn't just on the other track team members either; it was felt by many of the kids at Marshfield. After the County Meet students came to the audio visual room, like it was the Egyptian Theater, and paid ten cents to see the footage of the great race.

One day in late May, just a few weeks after the County Meet, I was working on some final stories that I wanted to go to print. I looked up from my small desk in the newspaper office, and in strolls the swim coach, Ralph Mohr.

"Hey there!" he greeted me. "I've read some of the stories you've written for our Pirate teams. Not a bad job, son." He stood over my desk and rested a hand on my shoulder. I was surprised he'd come to talk to me and compliment my work.

"I see you're a Prefontaine fan." He pointed to the two pictures I had pinned to my bulletin board.

"Yes, sir. I like to refer to them as 'Pre in motion'."

"Well, now." Coach Mohr pulled up a chair next to mine and sat with his arms folded across his chest. "Let me give ya a little story of my own about *Pre in motion*."

"Sure!" I grabbed my yellow tablet of paper.

"You won't have to write this down, you'll remember; just listen."

"O.K." I rested my pencil on top of the pad.

"I watched Pre compete at the County Meet. This being my first year here at Marshfield, I want to get to know as many of the students as I can. I don't know much about running and track times and all that. I'm the swim coach, right?"

I nodded and he continued.

"Well anyway, we all know that Pre ran the mile in 4:06. Seemed impressive enough to me, so I turned to Coach McClure and his assistant Phil Pursian and I asked them 'Is that a good time for a high school kid?' They just looked to one another as if I was crazy. The crowd was cheering..."

"I know, it sure was something, wasn't it?"

"Yeah," Coach Mohr laughs. "Only I didn't know it at the time!" Pursian said to me, 'Ralph, That's *record* time for a high school kid!'"

"And I can quote you on that?" I asked as Coach Mohr got up and tucked a purple cap on his head.

"You bet! And you can also print that I know a good runner when I see one now!"

Pre went undefeated in track and cross country in his junior and senior years. He set the national high school record for the two mile his senior year, coming in at 8:41.5. And set a personal best in the one mile, (4:06.0.) at the Golden West Invitational Meet in California. The participants were undoubtedly the top high school runners In the U.S. During his years as a Pirate, Pre broke a total of 19 national high school records. No one in Oregon had accomplished a lot of things Pre was getting ready to do.

Pre wasn't afraid of hard work, that's for sure; but something must be said for the devoted mentors he had in his coaches. It began at Marshfield with Walter McClure and his assistant Phil Pursian, and continued on at the University of Oregon with Bill Bowerman and his assistant Bill Dellinger. These men not only believed in Pre and his abilities, but helped him to focus all of his sometimes untamed energy. Pre understood at an early age that achieving success in his sport meant he had to be ready to give up some of the things other kids take for granted. He willingly made that sacrifice, but he had the love and respect of his coaches to convince him he had made the right decision.

There is a very vivid example of this unique kind of bond between coach and athlete - the story of Pre's time in Miami, the summer after high school graduation. This account was told to me by Coach McClure. And the rest was for all of Coos Bay to read about in our town newspaper, *The World*.

After his victory in the Golden West Meet, the AAU summoned Pre to run the 3 mile in their championships. One problem - the money for the air fair! The AAU wasn't offering any help in that department. Bill Huggins, father of Pre's fellow track member and good buddy Tom Huggins, took it upon himself to collect money from the townspeople. He soon had what was needed to get Pre to Miami.

Walter McClure accompanied Pre. When they were boarding the plane the ticket taker inquired "Hey Pre, are you going to Miami?" Pre's eyes were wide with surprise as he looked to his coach, and then back to the clerk.

"You know who I am?" he asked.

"Sure, anyone who knows anything about track knows who you are!"

Obviously the ticket taker was a track enthusiast as well.

This couldn't have tickled Pre more. Coach McClure hurried his young charge onto the plane. The two were scheduled to fly first to St. Louis, during which time Mac remembers that Pre had dozens of questions about flying for the bemused flight attendant.

During their stop-over in St. Louis, the travelers were greeted by a V.I.P representative who asked "Is this the Prefontaine party?" Pre flashed a rascally smile at Coach McClure. One can guess the young man's delight at being referred to as "the *Prefontaine* party!"

Finally arriving in Miami for a six day stay in preparation for the meet, the Prefontaine party was met by a friend of Pre's mother. The woman worked for a very wealthy family and offered to take young Steve on a tour of Miami and of the mansion she worked in. Pre's first (but certainly not his last!) question for his tour guide was "Can I bring my coach?" So Coach McClure got to come along and they toured a grand house, complete with lush gardens and a moat. Tethered alongside the bank was a boat, which was a welcome sight for a boy from Coos Bay, Oregon.

The day of the meet, Pre was raring to go. Once again he couldn't keep himself still as he waited for his time to race. It was June and the afternoon sun was bright and hot. Mac patiently coaxed his boy to calm down and save some of that energy for the race!

During the event an elderly couple from Naples, Florida sat next to Coach McClure. They had met Pre prior to the race and were sufficiently intrigued by the feisty young man. Mr. and Mrs. Thompson were on the edge of their seats as a remarkable race unfolded. With two laps to go Pre moved from 15th place (out of thirty runners), passing six, seven, eight runners on his way to the lead! When he was in sixth place Pre attempted to pass another runner who purposely gave him a hard jab of the elbow. In a gesture that was never done before, or repeated, Pre knocked his unsportsmanlike competitor clear off the track! Like all of us, Pre had some not-so-perfect moments, but he learned from them. He placed fourth in the race which qualified him to run for the national team in Europe later that summer.

A few days after the Miami meet, Mr. Thompson wrote to the Coos Bay newspaper *The World*. He and his wife wanted the town to know what they had witnessed - not only the talent and bravado of one young man, but the love and respect that ran between him and his coach, much like a river running through a mill town. *The World* printed the couple's letter, which ended with Mr. Thompson making a heartfelt observation about Pre and Mac. "We need more teams like these two." Coach McClure still has the article nestled among his treasured items - reminders of his days with Pre.

"I'll always love that boy," Mac said when he finished his account of their time in Miami. The emotion in his voice left me in no doubt of the fact.

As Pre's time at Marshfield was coming to a close, many colleges were chasing him down to run for their team. He made visits to several campuses, even going clear across the country to Philadelphia, Pennsylvania to check out Villanova University. He considered a college closer to home - Oregon State where a good number of his friends, including Tom Huggins and Fred Girt, were headed. Coach McClure was hoping Steve would choose his alma mater - the University of Oregon. Mac himself had run there. When Pre asked for his advice, his beloved teacher answered the question with a question. "Well Pre, where are all the runners?"

Amidst all the letters from schools enticing Steve away from Oregon, he wanted to receive just one note - something penned from the University of Oregon's esteemed Coach Bill Bowerman, who had trained many world-class athletes and was a legend of a man.

Pre already knew a good deal about the University of Oregon because of its reputation for producing some of the most notable track and field athletes; but that admiration ran both ways. Some of the university's current track team members would spend overnights at Pre and his friend Tom Huggins' homes. These college boys had heard about the tough Coos Bay workouts - running on the sand dunes, through the woods thick with trees and mud, and in hilly terrain. They wanted the benefit of the training young Pre and Tom had.

They soon learned that keeping up with the Coos Bay kids would not be as easy as they thought. This point was brought home one cold, November morning. Rain poured from the cloud-filled sky, pelting each of the runners with fat drops of liquid. The wind kicked up, blowing the rain into their faces. They were going to run the sand dunes. The boys pushed on for two miles, then onto the beach for another two. After these demanding four miles, the runners reached another stretch of dunes. A large pool of water lay directly in their path.

One of the tuckered out University of Oregon boys looked at Steve; sure they would be stopping.

"Hey, looks kinda deep out there, don't ya think?" the college kid observed a little nervously.

"Nah!" Steve waved his hand as if it was no big deal. "We do this all the time. Come on!"

With that Steve took off into the dunes, the water rising up to his chest.

No doubt it was tricky going, even for the self-confident Steve; but he wasn't about to give up. None of the college runners wanted to be outdone by a mere high school kid. So Steve led the charge onward, his plucky commitment assuring that no one else would give up either.

This sense of resolve was as much a part of Steve as his powerful legs. There were times when his strong will would kick in and that instinct to give his very best would take over.

One meet during his senior year, Coaches McClure and Pursian asked Steve if he would help the other runners by setting the pace during the first part of the race - hang back a little instead of going out full force. Steve agreed to their request. Half way into the race he sprang from the middle of the pack, opening up a 200 yard lead. No one could get near him.

After the race Phil Pursian asked him what had happened to their agreed plan. Steve replied with total honesty.

"I'm sorry coach, but one of the guys from another other school started mouthing off 'this Prefontaine kid can't be very good.' I just got so mad!"

He sure did. Steve ran a sixty second quarter mile that race.

Even with that strong will, Steve's track workouts sometimes pushed him to the limit. But it was the way he handled reaching the edge that taught us all a little something.

Steve would run 220 meters repeatedly - 12, 15, 16 times back to back with 100 meter jogs in between. Sometimes he would be so exhausted he'd say "I don't think I can run another one!" His coaches would tell him to leave it for the day and go take a shower. But Steve didn't hit the showers. He slowed his pace to a jog, finished the work out and would be back the next day raring to go.

On the way back from a meet in his senior year, Steve told Coach Pursian that he didn't feel sharp. "I need a good, hard work out," he insisted.

Pursian told Steve to meet him at the track the next morning, a Saturday. Coach was going to give the young runner not only a physical work out, but a mental one as well. He wanted to see how well Steve was able to judge his own time. When they met the next day, coach had him running 100 meters at different time intervals. Steve loved the clock, watching the time - his time. But was his internal clock a reliable one? Yes, indeed it was. No matter what time Pursian requested – 14.7, 16.2, 17, etc. - Steve would always come within one tenth of a second of the time. Then coach asked Steve to run a ridiculously slow time, something like 26 seconds. Steve could only throw back his head and laugh. "I can't run *that* slow, coach!" he declared.

I think of Steve as a man who took a road few of us travel. If he came across an obstacle in his path, he had a few choices. He could try and knock the obstacle out of the way - but what if it was too heavy to move? He could try and go around it - but what if it was too wide to pass? He could jump over it, but what if it was too high? He could turn around and just give up; find another, less taxing road

- but what would he have accomplished then? No, Steve was not one to walk away from a challenge. He would summon his incredible willpower and climb right over that barrier.

Steve also had a great sense of fun. I opened up the Coos Bay World newspaper one day, and whose picture did I see? Yes, it was Steve Prefontaine. He wasn't suited up in his Marshfield uniform, however. He wasn't setting a new county or state record. He wasn't running at all. Steve was standing still; a very rare moment for him. His hair was artfully slicked back and he was sporting some stylish shirts that a local seamstress had made. She asked Steve if he would be good enough to model her work. The pirate looked pretty impressive, even standing still.

A few days later I literally bumped into Steve, (actually, he crashed into me in his rush to get to class.)

"Ah, hey, I'm sorry 'bout that!" He took a moment to slow down and make sure I wasn't damaged. "You O.K.?"

"Yeah, no problem." I grinned, looking at my books that had landed on the floor like a stack of overturned pancakes.

"Pre! Come on! A bunch of us are ditching class to hang out in the park," one of Steve's friends called from the stairway. The bell was just about to ring.

"No way, man! I'm not missing Drafting. It's my favorite class!" He bent down to help me pick up my books. "You better get to class too," he said, as he handed over my English and Biology books and gave me a quick pat on the shoulder.

"Right." I straightened my glasses. "Oh, and uh, nice pictures of you in the World." I grinned.

"What?" He quickly realized what I was referring to. "Oh, that. It was just a favor for someone, you know..."

The bell rang and he carried on his way. Before he turned around though, I spotted a hint of devilment in his eyes.

Coach Bowerman's assistant, Bill Dellinger, had already seen Pre run and was convinced it was only a matter of time before the promising young man would run in the Olympics, just as Bill himself had done.

Coach Bowerman finally wrote, and Steve decided. He was headed to the University of Oregon, his winged shoes to touch down on the renowned Hayward Field. After Steve's acceptance, Bowerman - obviously very much taken with Prefontaine - wrote another letter. This time it was to the sports editor of the Coos Bay Times, and was in the form of an open letter to Steve, his family and the entire town of Coos Bay.

The last paragraph read:

"I want to assure the people of Coos Bay, the Prefontaines, and of course, the champion, that we are humbly aware of the great responsibility that we have to help this young man achieve his ambitions and goals, educationally as well as on the running track. I have every confidence that if he keeps his eye on the target, and his dedication, with his background and with the future, he will become the greatest runner in the world. There are many pitfalls along the way, but I'm sure that with the encouragement that he will get from the community everything that he has in mind can be accomplished.

My sincere gratitude, again to the entire community, and the individuals who made this young man's success possible.

Sincerely,
W.J. Bowerman
Track Coach
University of Oregon"

I had gained entrance into the University of Oregon by way of a writing scholarship. I was quite hopeful that my typewriter and I would be kept very busy, so long as I kept my eyes focused on Hayward Field.

3

Star Shine

I wouldn't be a very good sports reporter if I didn't tell you a little something about the AAU (The Amateur Athletic Union). I won't bore you with an elaborate history of the organization. The important facts are that it was established in the late 1800s to promote and develop amateur sports and physical fitness programs. But, as Pre would later observe, the amateur sportsmen of the 1800s were a lot different than the amateur sportsmen of his own generation. Back when the AAU was formed, its members were mostly wealthy people who were already well known and didn't really need any promotion or help. Pre would find out that dealing with the AAU was anything but simple or supportive.

Athletes like Pre could barely make ends meet with the tiny sums they received from the AAU. Meanwhile, athletes from European countries were treated like gold. They were given jobs that wouldn't conflict with their training and competition schedules, they didn't have to be concerned with having enough money to live, and they had a team of doctors and trainers to look after all their needs. If you were an Olympic hopeful living in Europe during the time that Pre ran for the US, you were considered a national treasure by your country. The AAU treated their American athletes as less than treasures - more like servants.

In 1969 Pre got his first taste of how the AAU did things. That same championship meet in Miami I spoke of earlier was the beginning of a very frustrating relationship between Pre and the governing body. The AAU decided which person would run in which race. Having scheduled Pre to run in the Miami race, they pulled him out of it at the last minute. And then, because it suited their purposes, they reinstated him. This kind of disrespect and disregard for an athlete is exactly how Pre's aggravating relationship with the AAU began and continued. Pre would grow more outspoken and active in demanding rights for all amateur athletes. He was the driving force for great change from which many athletes have benefited.

That's your short introduction of Pre and the AAU. Now we're off to the University of Oregon and the renowned Hayward Field.

It was the fall of 1969 when Pre headed to Eugene, Oregon. Six weeks before he had been running in European meets and hanging with some of the world's best runners, many of them much older and more experienced than him. It was there he ran his best time yet: 13:52.8 in the 5000 meters.

The distance between Coos Bay and Eugene is roughly 100 miles, give or take. But, whereas the Coos Bay of Pre's youth was a close-knit community made up of hard working, no-nonsense folks, the Eugene of Pre's emerging adulthood was a university town, a place where artists and students gathered. Although there were plenty of parks (about 100!) and over two thousand acres of open space to play, athletes were a strange breed to many of the people of Eugene. Pre was more than simply a kid with a track scholarship.

He was an athlete competing on the national and international levels at age seventeen.

The Aquarius did manage to settle near water, but the Willamette and McKenzie rivers weren't the familiar Mingus Park Creek or the Sunset Bay of his boyhood. Pre was entering new territory and, as any freshman in college will tell you, the unknown can be a little scary. Pre handled entering university life just like he did his sport, full on and ready to meet the challenge.

I mentioned that Pre's mother and grandmother were from Germany. No one can really know the fear and uncertainty they faced during those darkest years of the Second World War in their homeland. It seems to me that Elfriede and her mother must have come to the US feeling a little nervous, maybe wondering how people would view them and how they would be treated. Despite their difficult past, Pre's mother and grandmother were warm and loving people.

I've been thinking a lot about this and Pre. Maybe it was because Pre really understood what it would feel like to be unfairly judged that he was able to be so accepting of others. Maybe because he saw the fear in the eyes of those facing the unknown, he was able to see the unfamiliar with the eyes of a seeker. Maybe all the uncertainty and self-doubt in others convinced him of the need to believe in himself without question.

When Pre cruised into Eugene he wasn't pretending to be a great scholar or artist; he wasn't trying to be anyone other than himself - which is why a lot of students gave him a hard time.

"Would you look at that hick. Nice car."

My roommate Michael was snickering as he pointed to the blue Chevy with mag wheels parking in front of a row of downtown Eugene shops. Michael and I were just coming from the bookstore and my arms were loaded down with a semester's worth of reading. I didn't have a free hand to reach for my glasses to get a better look at who Michael was referring to. But I didn't need my glasses.

As we came closer to the car, I could see the windows were rolled down and heard the rock music playing on the radio. The driver switched off the engine, popped open a door and eased the keys into the pocket of his blue jeans. His T-shirt read *Hawaii Invitational*. He pushed some strands of hair behind his ear. The familiar blonde head looked from one end of the street to the other. His smile grew wider as he took in the scenery.

I wanted to stop and say something – felt, for some stupid reason, like I should welcome Pre to Eugene as if I was the town's ambassador of good will. Michael kept on walking. I'm sure Pre caught the condescending look my roommate offered as his only greeting. Pre turned his bright face to me as we passed.

"Hey man, good to see ya." He nodded.

"Yeah, you too." I juggled my books and returned the smile. "Have a great season," I called out over my shoulder.

Pre was still grinning, watching us move into the ocean of students and town's people. I'm sure he must have been in a hurry to get somewhere, but I remember feeling like he was right where he was meant to be.

"You know that jock?" Michael looked at me as if I had just greeted an alien.

I turned to him, angry and shocked at his stuck-up attitude. As if on cue, a book from my stack fell onto his foot.

"Yeah I know him." I let Michael stoop down and pick up the hardback poetry book. "His name's Pre and he's one heck of an athlete."

The Oregon Daily Emerald, the university's campus newspaper, is housed on the third floor journalism building in Allen Hall. I made my appearance there within the first two weeks of the semester, hoping for the opportunity to write about the Ducks (that's the name the sports teams were known by.) But, even though I had managed to get a scholarship for my writing, the Editor-in-Chief made it clear that I'd have to prove myself before any stories of mine would make print.

I was asked what department I'd like to write for, my "dream assignment." I answered without hesitation.

"Sports!"

"Any particular sport?" the editor inquired.

"Well, I'd really like to cover the track and field meets."

"*Track?*"

This seemed to come as a shock to him, although I couldn't imagine why. Hayward Field was the place where all U of O runners spent most of their time, and where past Olympic medalists had sweated at the start of their careers. They included Pre's new coach, Bill Dellinger who had won the Bronze in the 5000 meters in 1964. And Pre's head coach, Bill Bowerman - well, the man was no less than a legend, even then in 1969.

"There's a new guy, Steve Prefontaine. He's from my home town, Coos Bay." I stuttered. "I think he's really going to be somebody to watch."

"Prefonwho?" the editor shuffled some papers on his desk absentmindedly. "Never heard of him." He looked up with a blank expression. "But, O.K. I tell you what, if you want to write about this Pre... Pre..." He stammered trying to pronounce the full name.

"That's it exactly! It's Pre." I confirmed.

"If you want to write about him, be my guest. There's no guarantee that I'll print any of the stories, but at least I'll get a good idea of your writing abilities. And it'll show me if you can really stick with an assignment."

I smiled, thinking of the young man I'd be writing about. Somehow the challenge of sticking to the job seemed like a no brainier. I managed to hold back the "I'm with stupid" look I wanted to give the editor. I was just thankful for the assignment, or test as he chose to see it.

"Thanks," I said, doing my best to look like a genuine reporter. I thought about sticking a pencil behind one ear. "I really appreciate the opportunity."

"Oh, and I forgot to mention..." The editor was walking away from me now, imparting a final direction. "During the times you aren't writing about *Pre*, you'll be cleaning up this office. Trash cans always need to be emptied around here."

He flashed a sarcastic smile and left me standing there feeling like I had just been given the best job on campus. Like, I cared that

I'd have to empty a few trash cans for the chance to prove myself by writing about Pre.

It's been said that when Pre entered college, it was because of his Coos Bay innocence that he believed he could do anything he set his mind to. I'm not so sure of that, as I too came from Coos Bay; and when I went to the University I had a lot of doubts about myself. Being away from my family and home town, I began to question what I really believed in. The world was a crazy, unsure place to me.

I carried with me my suitcases, books, typewriter and a whole lot of uncertainty when I arrived at U of O. I think Pre always carried with him his family, friends and the simple yet determined attitudes of Coos Bay. This, I think, was part of what gave Pre his stubborn pursuit of excellence. Many times he clashed swords with Coach Bowerman, who had nicknamed Pre "The rube" on account of his running style. Pre was known as a "front runner" - someone who, from the starting gun, runs his fastest and hardest. He believed the person who sets the pace wins the race. He felt that holding back and coasting through most of a race, only to surge ahead in the end while other runners were giving it their all the entire race, was lacking courage. Pre said "A lot of people run a race to see who is the fastest. I run to see who has the most guts, who can punish himself into exhausting pace, and then at the end, punish himself even more."

But the other part that made up Pre was that indescribable something. How can I say it in words? It's like this: we all know it when we see it. Like how a person seems to light up a room when he walks in; or how, when you are with someone of that sort, you just know you are in the midst of something rare. Their eyes have a fire, a hunger. That's what Pre had; and it's like having an elephant in your living room. You can't hide it even if you want to. Pre had confidence and he wasn't ashamed of that, even though a lot of people thought he should be.

For example, one day I was walking with Michael across campus. We were getting to know where all the different dorms were - especially the ones that housed the girls. We took a wrong turn and ended up in front of a small complex of dorms that faced inward, towards each other.

I happened to look up and saw a pair of sweatpants hanging in a bedroom window. They had the letters "U.S.A" on one leg - the uniform of the national team. I couldn't help but laugh out loud. There was the pride and resolve hanging up for all to see.

"What *is* that?" Michael asked as his eyes followed mine to the window.

"Just what it says, a U.S.A. champ." I pulled him along.

For the first season I decided I would simply attend as many meets as I could and get to know Pre in and out as a runner - his style and so on. This was the beginning of a very important lesson for me, something that not even four years of college would teach me.

I was beginning to understand that the Steve Prefontaine I had witnessed during my youth - the boy who would not give up no matter what anyone else said or thought about him, the boy who had a generous and mischievous nature - was the very same bold, confident runner who took to the track each and every meet.

Too many people have different "faces" they show to the world, depending on who they want to impress. For instance, I wanted very much to be seen as the intelligent and excellent student by my teachers; as the spot on, talented writer by the editor of the newspaper; and as a cool and popular dude by my fellow students. Honestly, it gets hard accommodating all those faces in one person. Some days I just wanted to be Owen, if only I knew who *he* was!

Pre understood the delicate balance of being a much admired public figure and being a son, brother friend; a "regular guy". He held himself to a higher standard than most when dealing with his many fans and the media. He was respectful, gracious and always spoke the truth. Pre was aware that people looked up to him - especially kids, and he took that privilege very seriously.

But Pre was also able to be more relaxed and a bit of the mischievous Coos Bay boy when he was with his family and close friends. Pre, as I came to see, had a core of decency and sincerity that never fluctuated, whether he was on or off the track and no matter who he was with. Sure, he had some maturing to do as we all did. In fact, that first season at the ripe old age of 19, he had qualified once again to run for the AAU in an international competition. He was running in a 5000 race against West Germany. And, being Pre, he had no problem taking the lead and running the race full out from the word go. But with only one lap remaining, his West German opponent, having stored up his energy by coasting most of the race, made a calculated dash (or "kick" as it's called in the running world) for the lead and the win.

This ticked Pre off to no end. It would not be the first or last time that Pre would express the feeling that he didn't have much respect for runners (especially the older, more experienced ones) who would hold back in a race only to "steal" the win at the end, while others - like Pre - gave their all the entire race.

Coach McClure hoped that Pre would come to fully appreciate the things he had tried to impart at Marshfield. The most important being that Pre's time as a runner was just beginning. There were so many more accomplishments to come if he remembered that time and patience would take him where he wanted to go.

I wonder if Pre somehow knew he wouldn't have that much time to accomplish all that he wanted to, and this knowledge made him so driven. Pre's friend and fellow runner Fran Worthen said "When you're a runner, you seem to live your life in minutes and seconds, realizing how important each one is."

During one interview, after winning the three mile in under thirteen minutes, the question was asked "Steve, we watched you coming around here, and it looked like you had your eye on the clock the whole race. Is that true?" Steve brushed back the wet hair from his eyes and with a shy smile admitted "Kind of. That's my favorite time piece."

Pre was always Pre. When he ran he was speaking directly to you. He had no need for words. Words could have never explained all there was to him anyway. He ran holding nothing back. He showed his soul through his sweat and pain. Pre knew who he was and believed in what he was doing full on, from the word go.

Pre never went anywhere without thinking of, and making time for, running. As a college student, he would travel back to Coos Bay to spend time with his family. The Prefontaines would sometimes pile into the car to visit relatives who lived in the country. It would be a day-long outing, so Pre made sure to bring along his running gear. After a good meal and some downtime he would lace up his shoes, collect his sister Linda, and they would take off down the deserted country back roads.

Linda would drive the old car next to her brother while he ran. He'd let her know just what speed he needed her to drive at so he could maintain the required pace. Linda's window would be rolled down. She'd be ready to take directions, offer encouragement - and the occasional tease. This was usually met with her brother sticking his hand through the open window and ruffling Linda's long hair. What a pair! Pre trying to keep his steady pace and joke with his sister while she drove; and Linda endeavoring to keep the car straight on and rib her brother. These were particularly precious times for the two of them; times that would become increasingly rare as they grew older and into their adult lives. But they always remained as close in heart as they were in body during those country car rides.

Steve took on his first year of track at the University of Oregon with ease. He won the three-mile at every meet, including the Pac 8 Championships. What's the Pac 8 you may ask? It stands for the Pacific Eight Conference (although, at the present time there are ten schools that participate). It is a college athletic conference, and part of the NCAA (National Collegiate Athletic Association). Both are pretty big deals as far as college competition is concerned.

Many who knew Pre have said that he had the ability to push past the limits of physical and mental pain and run on sheer will. I believe that is true. Before a very significant race, (the NCAA Championship) during his freshman year, Pre had cut his foot pretty badly. He needed twelve stitches and, after only 24 hours on ice, he ran the three mile in 13:22.0. He didn't just finish the race despite his stitches being ripped open, he won. After that, not only I and the good people of Coos Bay could see how great an athlete Steve Prefontaine was; suddenly the whole world was waking up to the fact.

It was coming on summer of my freshman year. I was making one of the many pots of coffee that I would brew in my four years at the Daily Emerald. My editor came barging out of his tiny office. He was sorting the mail in his hands, and plopped a magazine dramatically on the coffee table in front of me.

"Did you see this?" he asked through gritted teeth.

I put down the coffee can and took up my glasses to get a look. The magazine was Sports Illustrated, dated June 15th 1970. On the cover was a young man, his face burning with resolution. He was running on a ridge not far from Head Coach Bowerman's home. He was wearing green and yellow – 'Duck' colors. His T-shirt read

Oregon. The caption next to the picture said *America's Distance Prodigy - Freshman Steve Prefontaine.*

"As I matter of fact, I..."

"And you didn't think it important to tell me this guy, Pre-fon-taine," my editor said, laboring the three syllables like he was leading a cheer. "... was a prodigy, for cryin' out loud?"

I did my best to hide my great satisfaction, offering patiently "I tried to tell you when I first started here, but..."

"But, nothing!" He grabbed the magazine again. "As of today I want you to cover every meet he runs in Eugene. In fact, I want you to cover everything he does here, running or not. Dig it?"

"Uh, sure." I couldn't hide my wide grin. "Does this mean you're going to print my stories?"

"Of course I'm going to print them! The guy is on the cover of Sports Illustrated! I think people will want to know about him."

"A little late for that," I said under my breath as the editor walked away in a huff.

"What's that?" he called over his shoulder.

"I said I think it would be *great* to do that!"

I forgot all about the coffee I was making and grabbed a notebook. If I was lucky maybe I'd catch Pre working out.

I did get to watch Pre working out many times. He viewed his workouts as seriously as he did his meets. His work ethic was so strong he would have run himself into the ground, had it not been for Coach Bowerman insisting that all runners (even Pre!) needed rest time. This rule was strictly enforced by the coach.

Some people accused Pre of being too proud because he would make predictions on what feat he would next accomplish. But his predictions were like promises. He always "walked the talk."

It was during rest times that Steve would catch up with his friends, visit with his family and do volunteer work.

Fred Girt, a young man who had attended Marshfield with Steve and knew him from their track days (Fred was a hurdler for the Pirates), recalls a time he got a big surprise while playing football for his college, Oregon State. His team was playing the University of Oregon at Autzen Stadium on the U of O campus.

"Some guy came up behind me during the game and started cheering real loud. He was urging me to show the people what Coos Bay boys are made of. I turned around and there was Steve wearing a University of Oregon letterman jacket and smiling from ear to ear. My teammates were all asking me, 'Who is that kid?' I said with pride 'That's Pre'."

Fred saw first hand how dedicated Pre was to his running, and how seriously he took his training. One night Fred paid a visit to Pre's fraternity house. Pre announced he had to leave the guys for a while to go running. He took to the streets of Eugene alone, rejoining his friends an hour later. Fred recalls falling asleep on the floor that same night. The house was full up. When Fred opened his eyes to the first flecks of sunlight, Pre was already up and out, taking in his morning run. "An easy ten," was how Pre always referred to the task. He'd come back, shower and make breakfast for his friends. Everyone else in the house slept in.

Steve wasn't just some hot shot out to make a name for himself. He cared about people and his team. Because Pre won the Pac 8 meet in California, he qualified to compete in the NCAA Cross Country Championships in Knoxville, Tennessee. But the Oregon track team as a whole did not; only Pre could go. The University wanted to send him, but Pre refused. He felt it was unfair to compete if his team members could not compete with him. The entire team did get to make the trip to Tennessee because of Pre's protest, and they won. Pre won a total of three NCAA Cross Country titles during his years at the University of Oregon.

In 1971 Pre won 21 straight College meets. That year he also won a gold medal in the Pan-Am games. By the time Pre and I completed our sophomore year, Pre went undefeated in cross country and I had written numerous stories about him. The people in Eugene were taking this intense young man from Coos Bay into their hearts; a victory he has held to this day.

When Pre took to the track at Hayward Field the cheering would reach a deafening level. Coach Dellinger recalls that he could not even hear himself speak because the atmosphere was saturated with the voices of so many, united in one mighty chant - "Go Pre!" Pre felt their support infusing him. It was like an electrical current passing back and forth between him and the crowd, "Pre's People" as they were known. Someone once remarked to me that being at Hayward Field when Pre ran was the closest thing to magic she had ever witnessed.

What exactly was that "magic"? As everyone knows, some mysteries cannot be explained. But I'm not talking the kind of spells familiar to Harry Potter. No, Pre's power was even more potent because it touched so many lives and exists today, more than three decades after his passing, like the dust of a falling star. There were some very real, notable elements to the power that Pre possessed and generously shared with others. I think Mary Paczesniak - long time Coos Bay resident and Pre fan - described it best when I spoke to her years after Pre's death.

"Pre and his fans were way ahead of their time. You need to understand that in the 70's Eugene was 'track town USA'. The people who came out to meets were very educated about track and field, and very appreciative of the hard work and effort that went into the great athletic performances achieved there. Pre's fans idolized him, and he them. I think Pre invented the "victory lap." Mary reflected.

"Hayward Field would be *packed* for all of its events and the fans understood what they were witnessing. There'd be the usual buzz happening in the stands, but as soon as Pre trotted onto the track for his warm-up everyone would stop talking and stare at him. They'd watch everything he did. And when Pre was actually competing, running lap after lap after lap, the section of the crowd he was running in front of would stand, clap and scream their support so loudly."

She stood up from her chair clapping and smiling as she demonstrated what went on during a U of O meet.

"They'd yell, 'GO PRE!' And then the next section of fans would stand, scream and cheer, etc. This would go on for his 13 or

26 laps, or whatever the length of the race he was running until everyone was on their feet stamping and cheering. It was incredible."

She closed her eyes for a moment as if she had been transported back to Hayward Field, hearing all the commotion and seeing Pre flashing down the track.

"You'd yell and yell and tears would be streaming down your face and it was because you knew you were witnessing something so special, something that couldn't be replicated by anyone else."

She opened her eyes and took my hands in hers.

"You know what I mean, Owen, a 26 lap race could get a little boring, couldn't it?"

I nodded, thinking back to the meets I sat through where Pre wasn't competing. To me, it felt like something was missing during those times. I said so to Mary.

"Oh boy!" she grinned. "Not so with Pre running. It was amazing. Talk about a home field advantage. His opponents had to be intimidated by all of that."

I knew exactly what she meant.

"And after his races were over, he'd jog those extra laps to express *his* appreciation to Pre's people for all they did for him. *We inspired him*! Isn't that great?" Her eyes were shining with the memory and emotion of it all. "It was just something," she finished in a hushed voice.

Many spectators have said that whenever Pre came out to run on what may have been a gray, overcast day, as if on queue the clouds would begin to lift and the sun ray's would slowly stretch across the sky as Pre stretched his arms and legs preparing to take flight.

There were so many victories on the track. I was kept very busy my last three years of college chronicling Pre's events. I made a scrapbook of all the stories I could find about him (even the ones I didn't write!) But I want to tell you a little more about the person of Pre. So much has been made about his excellence on the field, and rightly so; but that excellence, that sense of caring and child-like wonder of the world, the belief that all people have a gift and deserve to be encouraged - that's the Steve I'd like to tell you a little more about.

It was a difficult balance for me. I was on a mission of sorts to find out more about the boy I knew from Coos Bay, but my editor wanted me to write about the spectacular runner in Eugene. I had come to realize they were one and the same person. And those who only wanted to know (or thought they already knew) Pre just from his running accomplishments didn't have the full picture, as Tom Huggins once told me back in Marshfield. So I covered Pre's meets, and of course I was in awe of his athletic abilities like everyone else. But when Pre rested his insightful eyes on you, he was really seeing you. He was connecting with you, because he wanted that connection.

My editor thought I was simply covering track and field events, but I was also learning about what it truly means to be a person of conscience and not simply a "star."

"Pre has a big heart. He never forgets his friends."

That's what Tom Huggins said when I caught up with him for an interview a few years after we had graduated Marshfield. Tom was attending another Oregon college: Oregon State. He pointed out that, even with so many people wanting to talk to Pre - to get an autograph or shake his hand - Pre always made time for his friends. Tom attended several meets at Hayward Field and, despite the crush of strangers seeking attention from his friend, Tom was always greeted with warmth and sincerity by Pre.

I met up with Pre's childhood buddy Jay Farr to find out what he had to say about his friend and his great success. He wasn't surprised at Pre's accomplishments. Jay had witnessed the endless energy Pre possessed and his unshakable resolve.

"Pre has friends from all walks of life. And even though he is fiercely competitive in a race, once the race is over his competitors become his friends and he is happy to hang out with them."

This is what Tim Wall, another Coos Bay friend of Pre's had to say about Pre's rising fame.

"Pre is very loyal; he doesn't feel he's above the people of Coos Bay. He's almost reluctant to talk about his running achievements. Whenever he visits his friends, he wants to know how they are doing and what's going on in their lives. He doesn't think of himself as a 'big timer'."

And Jim Seyler, Pre's close childhood friend had this to say.

"Pre likes to give hugs. It doesn't matter if you are a man or woman. He's just a really warm person. When he's with you, he makes you feel like you are very important to him. He wants to know about *your* life, not talk about his".

And about Pre's hugs...they were well-known among his friends. Pre was known to give big, warm bear hugs. He wasn't afraid to show affection to his friends. Little sister Linda, who became a darn good tennis player and someone Pre was very proud of, went from being a young girl chased by her speed demon brother to sharing many hugs and memorable moments with him as an adult.

Sure, there were times when the spotlight must have gotten a little too hot and Pre needed some alone time. That's only natural. The Pre I came to know was a man who didn't just live for victory on the track. Pre always made time for kids especially. If he was preparing for a race, he spared some moments to speak with his youngest fans. After a meet he would stay for hours to sign autographs for the kids; oftentimes he would throw his shirt to them.

In 1970, after Pre's sub-four minute mile during an Oregon Twilight meet, Pre respectfully approached the stands to accept congratulations from the university president and his wife. As Pre balanced his small frame on the bleachers, he was surrounded on all sides by excited fans wanting autographs. I happened to be there, but I didn't want to crowd the athlete, so I stood slightly away from the clamoring group. I enjoyed watching Pre have a moment of appreciation. As he turned to the gathering of anxious autograph seekers his eyes caught mine. The smile on his face was as bright as a Coos Bay sunrise. He reached out over the heads in front of me to take my hand, shaking it warmly. "Thanks for coming," he yelled above the din.

Today I look back on who I was during the time I knew Steve. I marvel at the countless miles of travel and the many interesting people I've had the honor to know through the years. But it was a little fireball of a runner from my hometown, Coos Bay, Oregon - a man I had little direct contact with - who best showed me through his example how to be a real and decent person.

Roosevelt Junior High School was about a stone's throw away from the University of Oregon campus. The junior high was involved in a three year experimental, educational program when Pre walked through the doors and offered to volunteer his time. Despite his own school schedule, grueling work-outs and meets, Pre wanted to be with kids.

He was entering a school environment far different than what he'd been used to in Coos Bay. The philosophy of the Roosevelt program was, however, something he could appreciate. Its designers believed that teachers should be doing more than just getting their students to memorize facts, follow directions, and obey the rules.

The people at Roosevelt wanted to help their charges to become active learners. Students were encouraged to be creative, to think "outside the box", and learn on their own. Teachers were to be more like guides, rather than commanders of the learning experience. The kids could explore ideas, values, and relationships. They were encouraged to develop self-confidence, find the joy in learning, and not be afraid to ask "why?"

All of this must have been very appealing to Pre. But when he first came to the school, the faculty wasn't sure what to do with such a well known person as Steve Prefontaine. They couldn't very well have the super track star who packed Hayward Field to capacity serving up lunches, could they?

What the teachers at Roosevelt soon came to realize was that Pre would have been happy in the lunch room, on the playground, or in the classroom. He didn't act one bit like a "superstar." He was simply Pre, someone who had something to give.

In the beginning he had a small office where students could make appointments to talk with him. His schedule was booked solid with kids who wanted to sit and visit. The folks at Roosevelt quickly noticed that Pre could offer much more than a "come and talk to the athlete" role.

He was assigned to work with teacher, Ray Scofield. The students didn't address him as "Mr. Scofield" as would usually be expected. This was a different kind of school, so Mr. Scofield, was "Ray" to his students. Imagine calling your teacher by his first name! Weird, isn't it? Well, Ray taught English and he had a house. And I don't mean the place where Ray lived outside of school. I mean that he had a house *inside* school!

Each teacher advised a group of approximately 20 students made up of seventh, eighth, and ninth graders. House (like a "mega-homeroom") met for half an hour each day for announcements, attendance and so on - all the things that were part of a regular homeroom. But House was the heart of the Roosevelt program. It was meant to foster a working, active relationship between the students, their advisor-teacher and their parents. House helped students to understand from experience values like loyalty, friendship and self-confidence.

Ray's House was #34 and their motto was "We Shal" (spelled without the last "l" on purpose because of someone's spelling accident!) They called themselves "The Scorpions." It was Ray's job to motivate his House members, encouraging them to think for themselves. The ideal objective for the students was that they could learn the basic skills they needed in numerous and interesting ways. As with everything that was done in House, the students would vote to see if Pre could join. He had to plead his case as to why he would be a good addition. Far from being insulted by the task, Pre loved the challenge of convincing the kids to give him a chance. They did, and that's when some fun and valuable times for House 34 began.

There were some aspects of Pre's life as a popular athlete that could not be kept separate from his time at Roosevelt. Once the media in Oregon got word of Pre's work at the junior high, reporters wanted the story; and Pre unexpectedly taught the kids the grace of humility.

One lucky day while I was out grabbing some lunch, I spotted a reporter who worked for one of the Eugene Register Guard newspapers. He wanted the scoop on Pre at Roosevelt. The reporter knew what a big Pre fan I was, and asked if I'd like to come along. Of course I did. When we arrived at the school along with the photographer, I found out that Pre once again needed the approval of his House. He had to ask the kids to vote if they would allow the reporter and photographer inside the classroom to take pictures and collect information.

The kids voted in favor of the story seekers. That day a student from California was visiting the school, and happened to be in House 34 when the reporter, photographer, and I invaded. The flashbulbs were popping and the questions were coming fast from the eager press person. A question came from the back of the classroom that surprised us all.

"Hey," the boy from California called out. "Who's Steve Prefontaine?"

All eyes were on Steve, but the moment the question was delivered, Steve's smile was brighter than any camera flash and his laughter bigger and more joyful than any one of the kids' astonished chuckles. He got such a kick out of the fact that someone in that room didn't know who he was, other than just "Pre", a much-loved member of the House. I'm not sure of his exact words, but I think he said something like "Yeah, what's the big deal about this Prefontaine guy anyway?"

Steve took part in many of the House activities. When he committed himself to something, he meant it. He didn't just drop by from time to time and hang out, he got right in there with the kids and worked with them on whatever project they were doing at the time. He was instrumental in improving the intramural sports program for the House.

The Cross Country intramurals (as any intramural activity) were usually held during the House half hour, and therefore many of the Houses did not bother with the competitions, or showed lackluster turn outs. Steve's idea that everyone in House 34 show up for the activities, whether they participated or not (he called it "maximum participation for depth"), enabled the House to gain more points in these activities and gave the kids something to work towards. Steve's message to the kids was like an unforgettable song, playing over and over again in their heads, "Do your personal best every time you play!"

The kids responded to their "pied piper" by winning competitions; most importantly, they learned the value of just showing up every day and giving a little more than they had the day before.

Ray devised many activities to help with group building. Steve participated in these as well. He especially liked the physical games, such as "Break In."

I was assigned to write a paper for my child psychology class. I chose to write about the education program at Roosevelt. I was very pleased to be assigned to Ray Scofield's House (after they voted on the idea first!) to observe a day of activities. The House was playing "Break In" the day I came. I watched as three students made a circle facing outward, their hands firmly clasped together. A volunteer then tried to break into the circle by trying to unclasp two hands. If he or she was successful, the person joined the circle; if the student was not, a new volunteer would try.

The circle had grown to seven, strong-willed people. Steve sat on a desk top with his legs folded under him like the Buddha. He was shouting out words of support to the volunteers and the circle members.

"Stay strong! Keep it together, guys!" he called to the circle.

The kids' lips were tight lines of resolution, but their arms were getting weaker from all the tugging.

"Come on now, Mike, get in there! You can do it!" Steve urged the new volunteer. "Think how much you want to get in that circle!"

I looked to Steve, trying to hide my delight at seeing how heartening he was to all the kids. I didn't want him to think I wasn't taking my job just as seriously as the kids. He gave me a quick wink before he slid off the desk and became the next volunteer.

"Oh no!" The circle gave out a collective groan when Steve approached rubbing his hands together like a magician ready to pull a rabbit out of his hat. There was a definite twinkle in his eyes as he grabbed on to two of the kids' hands, attempting to make it in.

"Here I come!" he announced, giving a tug that was gentle enough not to hurt, but strong enough to gain him entry and end the game. Eight circle members was the limit. "Well now, we have to start all over again!" He held the student's hands in the air like a victory wave after a race. And sure enough, three new volunteers made another circle.

I kept my head down, pretending I was taking notes. I was afraid Steve might call on me next!

A month after my classroom visit I received a newsletter from Roosevelt High's House 34 in my mail box. There was a smiley face drawn in the lower right hand corner, and the second paragraph was underlined in red pen. It read:

We've climbed Spencer Butte twice this fall in search of the ghost — both times at night. The first time a parent and I accompanied the group along the moonlit trails and through patches of poison oak, while the second time Steve Prefontaine (an older House member) and I led the group, which was attacked by a "ghost."

After so many fruitless searches for the ghost, a former House member put on an unplanned spectral demonstration on the summit. It succeeded in sending one House member (who shall remain nameless) screaming for cover while the rest of us stood there courageously horrified! Later we all said that we knew what it was all the time, and swore that we were never fooled for a minute.

"Ha!" I laughed outright. I knew all about that ghost hunt. I was there, and I can tell you exactly what happened.

One of the most beloved activities for House 34 was climbing Spencer Butte in order to do some "ghost busting." I'd say the Butte is likely one of the most popular landmarks in Eugene. Lots of people who live in the town and beyond have made the trek up the steep trail. During a hike you are treated to a lovely forest view, as there are many fir trees lining the way. The top of the Butte sits above the tree line and is made up of rock formations. Besides the supposed supernatural dangers, there are also natural ones to look out for, like rattlesnakes, the steep and muddy trail, and poison oak!

After my day of classroom observation I was invited to come along on one of the Butte climbs. I think Pre may have pleaded my case to the kids in order to give me that chance.

We started our climb after sunset, armed with flashlights, warm coats and food to sustain us for any ghostly encounters. Pre was flanked on all sides by kids as we climbed. He chatted easily. Sometimes he'd hum a song and challenge his peers to "name that tune."

The first thing to do upon arrival was to locate the container with the note that described what happened during the last visit. Each time a group from House 34 climbed the Butte they would leave a written account of their trip and all present would sign their names. Depending on the amount of light (or lack thereof!) and availability of paper, these notes could be pretty cryptic. The missives were well hidden, usually behind patches of rocks. This was the keeping of Butte history. It was considered a great honor to take part in the ritual. Pre seemed to really enjoy the mysterious element of the secreted notes.

Once we settled in on a rocky ledge of sorts, we broke out the M&Ms, fruit, potato chips, and Gatorade. Pictures were taken by Ray to capture the event. When I look at those photos now, of Pre surrounded by the wide-eyed faces of children, I can't believe that the young man who could bring an entire stadium to its feet, cheering and screaming his name as he broke yet another track record, was the same man looking into the camera with such expectant eyes. His expression was that of anticipation, a "what's going to happen next?" grin. Pre was as natural a part of that gathering of kids as the trees were to the Butte.

In contrast, I remember how uncomfortable I was. I tried to put on a brave face, but all the time I was wondering just how close the rattlesnakes were (I found out later I was safe, being that the slithery creatures den after sunset) or if I happened to be sitting in a patch of poison oak. But Pre was in the moment - laughing and carrying on, having as good a time as any of the junior high kids.

Time passed and we all took out our slips of blue cellophane which Ray said were necessary in order to view any visiting ghosts. We held the flimsy material to our eyes and I could see Pre, his animated eyes covered by the blue stuff, lurking around and trying to give a little scare to his fellow hikers. The kid's laughed and the moon rose higher in the sky.

The transistor radio we'd brought along was broadcasting white noise. It was believed that the static indicated ghostly activity in the vicinity.

"SHH!!!" somebody warned in a hushed whisper.

"What's that?" Pre cried out, pointing towards the sky.

Slowly, a floating, yellowish apparition appeared dead ahead. It hung silently in the air. Before any of us could register what we were seeing, the hush was breached by the sound of short, successive blasts. There was a collective jolt as the kids scrambled with their cellophane, wondering aloud if they really were being invaded by ghosts. One girl was so frightened she began to scream and shake. Pre and Ray quickly took hold of her, trying to calm her down. They were very close to the Butte's south edge. One wrong move would have sent them on a nasty tumble to the rocks below.

It was soon discovered the sights and sounds were not out of this world, but of some older House members (now high school students) who had come back to set off fire crackers in an effort to frighten the others. It sure did work! The so-called ghost was really a garbage bag filled with air and a flashlight shinning from inside the sack.

I acted as if I knew what was going on the whole time of course, even though I, like the young girl, wanted to cut and run. Eventually she was convinced that everything was fine and her panicked question of "What if they are drug-crazed hippies come to shoot us?" set Pre to laughing big time.

That's what I remember most about that night, Pre's laughter blending with the shouts and giggles of the kids. I'm sure his voice was the loudest of all.

Speaking of Spencer Butte, there was another junior high school in Eugene, and that one was named for the place. Steve spent some of his time there as well. One of Steve's teammates, Pat Tyson, was doing his student teaching in Social Studies at the school. Pat asked Steve to come talk to the kids during assemblies. Nothing really formal; Pat suggested Steve talk about running, working hard, having goals - stuff Steve was very familiar with. Even so, before his first lecture, Steve was concerned that the kids might not be interested. Getting up in front of a bunch of junior high kids (who know everything about everything anyway!) was a little intimidating.

But he stood in front of his audience and kept it real. All eyes were glued to him, and you could hear a pin drop as he spoke. The students were impressed with Steve's honesty, passion, and obvious sense of caring.

Tracy Hickman, a student at Spencer Butte and a member of Pat Tyson's class, got an awesome opportunity few of us ever do. Tracy and Pat struck up a friendship of sorts. They were both very interested in current events and history. The student admired his teacher, and he was also a huge Pre fan. When Tracy found out that Pat actually knew Pre and was even friends with him, the boy was astounded. He invited the two college teammates to join him at his home for dinner with his parents. Pat and Pre accepted.

The thirteen-year-old host could hardly touch his food. He was so amazed that a celebrity like Steve Prefontaine was in his house. Tracy was your typical starry-eyed teenager. Imagine if you had the chance to not only meet the person you idolized most, but to have that person to your home for dinner! Yep. That's how Tracy Hickman felt too. He soon found his voice though, and began to ask Pre all kinds of questions. The young man wasn't a runner, he lIked ball-sports. He wanted Pre to tell him what it was like being famous.

Mr. and Mrs. Hickman were afraid their son was making their dinner guest a bit uncomfortable with his probing personal questions. But Pre, in his well mannered way, assured the parents it was O.K. for Tracy to inquire. He wanted to explain both the positive and negative sides to fame.

Tracy thought if a person was famous, that person was automatically rich as well. It was important to Pre that the boy understood what the AAU was doing to all the hardworking Olympic hopefuls in the US. Pre explained that, because of the way amateur sports were being conducted (by the strong arm of the AAU) any American athlete who dreamed of participating in the Olympics Games was far from rich. It didn't matter how hard an athlete trained, he did not have any rights as far as who he competed against or where he could compete. An athlete could not accept more than the few dollars a day and the minimal travel expenses the AAU granted. If he did, he would then be considered "professional" and the AAU would sanction him, thus killing his chances of ever participating in the Olympics. Meanwhile, the AAU was making a great deal of money from the box office sales of the meets they organized, using athletes who were commanded to participate.

Tracy was impressed with Pre's zeal on the subject of athletes' rights. He realized it must be a pretty tough situation to be at the top of your sport, making other people a lot of money but not seeing any of that money yourself, and not having a voice in your own athletic destiny.

"He was cool," Tracy said of Pre. "He treated me with respect. He talked to me like I was an adult. He was really intense and focused. Like, I knew when he smiled, it really meant something."

The young student had the chance to see Pre smile and make others smile as well. Pat and Pre took Tracy to a University of Oregon basketball game since the boy was such a great fan of the sport.

One thing that impressed Tracy was seeing first hand how popular Steve was. He didn't have too many moments to himself.

Someone was always coming over to say hello, to shake his hand, just to have a chance for a few brief words with their beloved hero.

"I was in awe of the whole scene, because I got to see for a moment what it was really like to be Steve Prefontaine," Tracy remembers. "Even though I knew it must have been frustrating to have people constantly coming up to him, he took time for each of them. I understood then what he meant about the positive and negative sides to fame."

The young Hickman also experienced the fun side of Pre too.

"He could do things, say things, that would make everybody laugh. He would just come out with these things; like if somebody was acting the big shot, Pre would call 'em on it. But he always spoke the truth, that's what was so great. He spoke the truth, and it might have made some people mad, but they knew he was just being honest. So what could they do but laugh too? They couldn't catch him if they tried!"

Tracy Hickman summed up his time with Pre like this:

"To me, Steve was bigger than life - a hero before I met him. And if I'd never had that chance, I would still feel that way about him. But having the experiences I did made an even greater impact on my life.

Today that young, starry-eyed student has grown into a man with three kids of his own. You can be sure they all know who Steve Prefontaine is and the very significant contribution he made in his short lifetime.

I could never have guessed that my reporting on Steve would challenge me to examine how I saw and thought about others. Once again, as a result of getting to know more about him, I got to know more about how things should be rather than how they are.

Steve volunteered his time not only with kids; he also worked with inmates at the Oregon State Penitentiary. These men once had dreams and goals but, for reasons as different as each man, they had let go of their dreams, made the wrong choices and ended up in prison.

I must admit, when I first learned that Steve was volunteering at the Penitentiary, I was unsure of how I felt. I thought anyone in prison must belong there. I wondered what could be done to help such lost people.

Steve knew. He knew these men needed to believe in themselves, and have someone to believe in them. Steve's sociology professor impressed upon his students that the inmates were not less than human because of the crimes they may have committed. Some of the men may have felt they could never accomplish anything but trouble. Steve could and would teach them a way to be better, a way to find dignity and self-worth within the walls that kept them separate from society.

That way was through running. Steve spent a good deal of his time helping to establish a running program at the prison. As you can imagine, not a lot of people wanted to assist this population and the inmates were most grateful to Steve for his attention and efforts.

Running gave the men an outlet - a chance to express their emotions in a positive way. And yes, they still have a track in the open area of the Penitentiary. The men take their running very seriously. What little money they make they use to buy their own running shoes through the prison commissary. They have their own competitions. The inmates look forward to each event, and the opportunity to show how practice and commitment will lead to improvement.

Steve took the time to explain the basics of running, such as technique, the importance of good footwear, the most beneficial exercises and so forth. He taught by his example, by the caring and respect he showed them as fellow human beings. Steve didn't judge, but worked with the men towards a common goal. Because of the respect he gave the inmates, he instilled in them a sense of respect for themselves and for others.

Thirty years after his death there are inmates who still remember Steve and what he did for them. Steve is a powerful part of the inmate consciousness. They talk of their gratitude to him, and they show respect to the people from the outside that come to run with them. Now, even women runners come to the penitentiary to work out with the inmates. Those inmates who knew Steve remember his inspiring example; and those men who never got the opportunity to meet him have come to learn about his gift from their elders. Steve left his everlasting imprint, a message of hope - that in order to receive respect, you must first give it. All people, no matter where they may be in life, impoverished and homeless or privileged millionaires, are equal when it comes to deserving the chance to make a change - to be better, and to achieve more by believing in themselves.

4

Miles to Fly

Pre spent his last two years of college racking up the records and victories, and gaining momentum towards the ultimate athletic competition: the Olympic Games.

Although he held celebrity status (one of his teammates, Mac Wilkins, called Pre "World" - short for "World Famous") during the time he was preparing for the 1972 Olympic Games. Pre by no means lived the glamorous life. He was limited as to what kind of employment he could acquire because of AAU rules regarding how much income their athletes were permitted to earn. If this wasn't restrictive enough, the AAU doled out a measly sum of $3 a day to cover travel expenses. This forced Pre to rely on food stamps, and he took in a roommate to cut the cost of living expenses.

He shared his trailer in Eugene with Pat Tyson, the Social Studies student-teacher who was also Pre's fellow U of O track team member. Pat remembers that Pre always kept their small home neat and clean. Pat was happy to live with Pre in the trailer that sat next to the Willamette River, because the rent was cheap and, more importantly, Tyson knew he would be training with the best track people in Oregon. Pat believed if you train with the best, you can become the best. He was right. He went on to coach both high school and college track and field, and is now one of the most well respected coaches in the nation.

Back in 1972 though, Tyson was just another struggling college student like Pre. Their living conditions were far from ideal.

The land around them didn't offer much of a beautiful view. They were surrounded by used car lots, machine shops, parking lots, and other trailer parks. But their lives had a rhythm much like their running. Pre was up and out the door at 6 am for a 35 minute run. He'd come back, shower, make breakfast - usually French toast or pancakes which he loved to top off with maple syrup and peanut butter. He took his vitamins, and was off to campus.

Pre never missed a class or an assignment. It was very important to him that he get everything done. He valued being able to talk with his professors and ask questions, especially about photography and design. Just like at Marshfield, Pre was always the first at track practice and the first to leave. He didn't believe in wasting time. As a matter of fact, Pre was a master at doing several things at one time - "multi-tasking" we call it now. Pat told me that Pre would be answering fan letters (he answered every letter he received), eating a sandwich while the T.V. was going, and he might take a phone call too! Pre loved the simple things. He and Pat would regularly visit one of the bakery thrift stores on Wednesdays and buy ten loaves of bread for $1. The thrift store had a "Wheel of Fortune" type game; any customer who spent over $1 could spin the wheel to win fruit pies, Ding Dongs, Snowballs, Twinkies, Hostess cupcakes etc. The two runners could load up on their sweets and carbs for next to nothing. And, speaking of sweet treats, Pre treasured the two-for-one banana splits at the Dairy Queen.

At night the two would head out to The Paddock, a local gathering place, and Pre would talk with everyone there. He didn't sit still for very long, but he'd never ignore someone. He held a person's eyes when he spoke to them, but eventually the temptation of competition called him away. He was always up for a game of air hockey, or arcade games like Frogger and Pong.

I think Pre was so well loved because he made the most of every moment in life and what it could bring. Pre gave people joy, because he made them feel special, important. He didn't judge people, because he didn't like to be judged. He knew where he came from, and that some people had it better than him, and some had it worse. That didn't make a difference to Pre. He could talk as easily with a biker as he could with a college professor. When you were around Pre, you couldn't help but feel *alive*! Pre's irresistible life force infected others.

Pre's life became a lot fuller when he focused all his time on training for the Olympics. He had said in an interview "If you're a runner, you're never completely satisfied unless you get a world record." But an Olympic gold would also be very satisfying to Pre.

Eugene, Oregon had the distinct honor of hosting its first ever Olympic Track and Field trials. This took place in July of 1972. The town was packed with athletes and spectators from around the world. I could hardly make my way through the downtown streets, they were so clogged with people. One little store seemed to be busier than the rest. It was called Blue Ribbon Sports. Do you recognize the name? I wouldn't expect you to. It was a new business back then. Later the store would grow and take on a new name – "Nike", after the Greek goddess of victory. Are you seeing a swoosh now? Pre's coach, Bill Bowerman, was one of the co-founders of the company and the creator of the feather-light, waffle soled running shoes - that he literally made from his own waffle iron! Pre would become the face of Nike.

Pre had been working harder than ever to build his threshold of pain and endurance. Not only did he intend to beat George Young at the Olympic trials, but Pre had set his sights even higher. He intended on running the last mile of the three mile or 5,000 meter Olympic race in four minutes or less. If he made the team, Pre would be going up against the strongest, fastest, and most experienced runners in the world. He was only 21 years old. If successful at the trials, Pre would be the youngest man running for the gold.

Pre's coaches, Bowerman and Dellinger, designed a training regime that was intended to build Pre's maximum effort late in the race. They began working to plan for that last exhausting mile. The work-outs were so specific and difficult that Coach Dellinger had to enlist the help of other track team members to run with Pre on different parts since no one person could keep up with him the entire way.

I sat in the empty bleachers of Hayward Field one warm summer afternoon. I was allowed to come to practices because of the stories I had written. I think I was someone to be trusted because I never tried to barge in on Pre's time by trying to get him to answer twenty questions, and I never misquoted him as so many other reporters had. I was a quiet, respectful observer. That's how I liked to get the information for my stories. After seeing how disrespectful the press could be, I vowed never to act in a way that I would be ashamed of. I'm sure Pre's message of finding your gift and doing your very best was sinking into my head without my even being aware of it.

I watched intently as Pre started in on his last work out of the day. It was two back to back beastly runs. Two other team members were helping out by running with Pre as the mid-day sun warmed the surface of the track. Pre bravely kept up the pace of his first run, but it was obvious that he was struggling towards the finish. I couldn't imagine what it would feel like to be out on the track day after day, pushing each time to the point of exhaustion and beyond.

Coach Dellinger - who I hoped was going to insist that Pre take the rest of the day off - watched as Pre dug in deeper. Coach knew better than to suggest that Pre take a break. In fact, Dellinger said he believed Pre's greatest accomplishment was the fact that, for four solid years, Pre never missed a practice or meet. Dellinger recalls that when he told Pre this, Pre responded "Well, coach, there were quite a few Saturdays when I didn't feel like coming to practice, and a few meets when I had a cold or sore throat. I knew you wouldn't let me run if I told you, so I didn't."

Dellinger had never seen such unwavering dedication in any of his athletes.

Before he could have the chance to run in the Munich Games, Pre first had to qualify. He had to defeat the three-time Olympian, George Young. I'd say there must have been close to 23,000 people in the stands at Hayward Field that day. I don't think anyone was sitting as Pre opened up with about two laps to the finish. People were cheering "Go Pre!" and proudly wearing the popular chant spelled out on their yellow and green T-shirts. As a gag, someone had made another T-shirt which read "Stop Pre" inside of a red stop sign. One of Pre's opponents was wearing the eye-catching shirt during warm-ups. I looked around and saw that a few other people in the stands were wearing the same. Most of the crowd, however, reacted by booing when they saw the shirt. I wondered: would Pre take this as a joke, or would he be insulted?

"What do ya think of that?" my roommate shouted to me over the thunderous crowd and pointed at the shirts in question.

"I don't think it will make much of a difference!" I yelled back.

"Oh no?"

"No way! I've seen his workouts. It would take a freight train to stop him!"

"We'll see..." My roommate loved to tease.

I didn't answer. Like Pre, I had my eyes on the clock.

No one could stop Pre that day. He literally ran away from George Young and everyone else. He broke his own American record with a new time of 13:22.8. In true Pre spirit he ran, sweating and exuberant. He grabbed one of the "Stop Pre" shirts from a person in the stands, put it on and took his victory lap. The crowd went crazy. If he hadn't thought the T-shirt funny at first, he made a great show of humor over it afterwards.

"What do ya think of *that*?!" I yelled to my roommate, clapping wildly.

Pre was off to Munich, but I would have to stay behind. I didn't have the money to make such a long distance trip. My editor said he wished the newspaper could afford to send me for the full report, but there wasn't enough in the budget.

"Don't worry. I'm sure you'll get a great story when Pre comes back to Eugene," my editor said, trying to cheer me.

But I wished I could be part of the excitement. I was sure I could have written one heck of a story. I didn't know then that a terrible tragedy was going to happen during those Olympic Games. After it was over I wondered whether I would have had the same courage to write, as Pre had to run.

Some of the events I'm now going to tell you about I saw on the television, like so many other people around the world. Some of the facts I learned after the Games. I continued to talk with people who were close to Pre in order to get a better understanding of what his experience would have been. I'm very grateful to Pre's friends for sharing with me. I can tell you what I've learned, but the biggest lesson for me was that I'll never truly know what Pre was thinking or feeling during his time in Munich. What I am sure of was that I saw one of the gutsiest races of my life, during what must have been the most difficult of times to run.

The Games opened with a lot of hoopla on August 26th, 1972. Pre and his teammates settled into their apartments, which gave a good view of the Israeli team's balcony.

They had draped their country's flag over the ledge. Bill Bowerman, head coach of the US Olympic Track and Field team, had made a point of speaking up about the lack of security in the Olympic village. Having been in the military, he had good sense about this kind of thing. He was told by the Munich Organizing

Committee that these were intended to be the "Happy Games", and that they did not wish to upset or worry anyone with too much police or security presence.

The Games proceeded and Finland's Lasse Viren was proving to be the competitor who concerned Pre the most. During one of the first track events Viren tripped and fell, but he got up and won the 10,000 meters - setting a world record. Viren would be running the 5,000 meters along with twelve other men, one of whom would be Steve Prefontaine.

But something happened before that race that would change the lives of many people. Sadly, Bill Bowerman's call for more security was about to be vindicated; but it had been ignored. In the early morning of September 5 eight members of a terrorist organization broke into the Israeli athletes' apartment, killing several of the team members and a coach. They took nine others hostage.

For an entire day Pre and the rest of the athletes waited anxiously in their apartments for news that the hostages would be freed and the terrible event concluded. Unfortunately, the hostages were killed in a failed rescue attempt by the German authorities. Twelve Israeli athletes and coaches lost their lives. The terrorists were also killed by their own explosives.

The Games were suspended. Each athlete searched his or her own conscience, seeking the answer as to whether they should, or could, go on competing. Pre was devastated. Bill Dellinger came to the Olympic village, hopped a fence and took Pre out with him. They spent a day in Austria where Pre went running, trying to regain his focus. Coach Dellinger, knowing how upset Pre was, took him back to his apartment instead of returning to the village. Pre agonized over the value and meaning of what he was trying to do. How important could winning an Olympic gold medal be when viewed against the deaths of twelve innocent people? Bill did his best to convince Pre that, if the Games were to be continued, he should take part. If they were cancelled, or if Pre decided to drop out, it could be said that the terrorists had won.

After a 34 hour delay, the Games resumed. The Olympic Committee decided that the Games should continue and be dedicated to the Israeli team. Calling them off would leave only an abiding memory of the atrocity. Many of the athletes agreed, since it would mean that the spirit of sport, not war, would be remembered.

Despite his mixed feelings, Pre decided to compete. But the memory of what he had witnessed would deeply affect him, not just in the immediate days following the attacks, but for a long time after he returned to the US.

There were a lot of things working against Pre as he stepped to the line on the day of the 5000 meter race. First, his feelings about the attack; second, the way some of the competitors ran – blatantly elbowing or spiking their rivals to get ahead, or boxing them in so they couldn't pass. Also, because the race was delayed, some of Pre's challengers had gained extra time to rest. And lastly, at 21 years of age Pre was the youngest runner in the competition. This was his first Olympic Games. All of the others had more experience and were in the prime of their running careers.

Despite these difficulties, Pre had made the prediction that he would run the last mile in under four minutes. He told one of the

American sportscasters "I'm going to work so that it's a pure guts race at the end. And if it is, I'm the only one who can win."

Pre had the support of his parents who had gone to Germany to cheer on their son. They were very proud of how far Pre had come. Ray and Elfriede knew Pre deserved to be in Munich because of his countless hours of sacrifice.

The folks in Eugene and Coos Bay were gathering together around televisions like one big extended family. The kids from House 34 sent Pre a Western Union telegram; it was simple, to the point, and what many others were saying as well, "GO!"

Michael, my roommate, and I joined a full table at the overflowing Paddock Tavern in Eugene where a great many of Pre's friends and admirers had come to watch the race. We were cheering before the event began. But as each runner took his mark, the room fell completely silent for the longest moment. It was like we were all taking a collective breath with Pre.

The runners were off - not like rocket fire, more like a slow, intentional flame. The 5000 meters was known as "the thinking man's race" because of the distance and the different strategy each competitor would use to break his opponents and win.

Pre never liked runners who thought too much. His strategy was to take control from the get go. But his competitors had other ideas. They maintained an unusually slow pace so as to conserve energy for the final few laps. Elbows and spikes were used liberally to keep runners who may have wanted to go out ahead in their place. They were like a single, evenly spaced line of men playing follow the leader. It was obvious that Pre was being boxed in -

trapped in the middle of the pack. He didn't like waiting for an opening. He didn't like it one bit.

We at the Paddock weren't too worried. We knew Steve would find a way out. One look at the fire in his eyes, even being translated to us by a television screen, showed the tenacity brewing within him.

All those watching, including the sportscasters, were becoming more nervous with the turtle-slow race. They commented that such an ambling pace could not continue for much longer. Someone was going to have to make a definite move.

"And Steve Prefontaine is going to take the lead! One mile, four laps to go!" the announcer was almost shouting in his excitement.

We were on our feet - some folks were standing on chairs - cheering as loudly as any crowd at Hayward Field. Pre had found his opening and was taking off. Lasse Viren, who had claimed he had no strategy for the race and was simply going to wait until something happened, waited no more and challenged Pre for the lead. It was an intense battle between the older policeman from Finland and the younger student from Coos Bay, Oregon.

My eyes were locked onto the television, but at the same time a flash of memory sparked in my mind. The little boy so intent on making beautiful pictures, letting no one interfere with his concentration, had been transformed into a young high school student bringing his focus with him onto the track at Marshfield High School - the beloved, rascally pirate. And then I saw him as the college student who enchanted thousands of people with his open heart, both on and off the track. All of these images were of the same person who was now running for his Olympic life against the best in the world. I knew in that moment as I watched Viren and Pre battling it out that, no matter what happened in this race, to me Pre would always be the best in the world. And not because of his athletic abilities, but because of *how* he ran and who he was as a person; how he gave of himself so totally, just like he ran.

"Pre is running a gutsy race. What a show he's putting on!" The other announcer was almost cheering himself. The admiration in his voice was obvious.

Mohamed Gamoudi of Tunisia moved up and suddenly the race was between three men: Viren, Pre and Gamoudi. When I think of that race, I'm still astounded that out of twelve men considered the greatest milers at that time, men with more familiarity of world class competition and with much more support from their respective countries, Pre was running out in front of them. He didn't let anything or anyone undermine his confidence. He had no need for strategies or game plans. As far as he was concerned, he was there to give his greatest effort. And that he did. He ran at the head of the pack, giving those "experienced" men cause for concern. No man -

not Viren, Gamoudi, Bedford - was going to take an easy victory, not with Pre's doggedness.

"Pre is showing all the guts in the world."

The commentator could barely be heard over the shouting in the tavern. We didn't need to hear him. We knew that Pre had the guts; we hoped he knew we were all right there with him, believing in him. Viren had edged out in front once again.

Pre made one last move down the back strait to regain the lead, but Viren was right there with him, Gamoudi too.

My roommate grabbed my arm, gripping it like it was the last life preserver on a sinking ship. "Go Pre!" I never heard him yell like that for anything or anyone.

Pre had given every last bit, straining for the finish line and the gold. He held on gallantly, staying shoulder to shoulder with Viren and Gamoudi. But in the last few yards, Pre had nothing left to give. It was Viren who broke away to cross the finish line first, then Gamoudi for the silver. As Pre staggered on with his final once of energy, he was passed by Ian Stewart of Great Britain who came out late in the final few paces to claim the bronze. Pre had run the last mile in 4:02, just two seconds behind Viren.

We stood in the Paddock in a respectful silence. No one in that room could move or speak. I can't remember what the announcers were saying then. Maybe someone turned off the television, I just don't know.

Michael still had hold of my arm. I looked at him, waiting for his snide comment. I couldn't think of an equally cutting reply. But his eyes were kind - sad, really. He squeezed my arm again and said

"I don't think I've ever seen anyone give a more valiant effort. You should be really proud of Pre."

I was. We were so proud of Pre. None of us was disappointed in him, but we felt as if we had somehow failed him. I recall there was one concentrated, communal emotion of wanting to give back to Pre all he had given to us. Now was the time he needed reassurance, a hug; and everyone who had been touched by Steve, even in the slightest way, wanted to touch back. "Pre's People" wanted him to know he was still a winner in our eyes. There would be other days, other races and we would be there, standing on our chairs and yelling at the top of our lungs "Go Pre!"

After the race, Pre escaped to the quiet, cool area underneath the stadium. He stood barefoot and tired. The constant stream of energy had ceased to flow. He didn't want to see or speak to anyone.

Blaine Newnham, sports editor of the Register Guard discovered the forlorn Pre. Something inside, not a reporter's instinct but that of a fellow human being, gave Blaine the courage to approach the disconsolate young runner. Blaine tried to reassure him. Pre wasn't looking for cheering up. He insisted he had nothing to say and started to walk away. But Blaine wouldn't give up. He realized how important it was in that moment to reach out to Pre.

He called after the athlete, insisting they should talk, and caught up with him. With his questions and comments, Newnham was able to get Pre to realize that, given his young age and this being his first Olympic appearance, he hadn't done so badly by placing fourth. Blaine was able to do what all of us back in Oregon wanted to, which was to give Pre that much needed hug. The writer managed to do that with his words of encouragement.

After a few moments of conversation another of Pre's competitors, David Bedford of Great Britain, walked by. A not so powerless Pre called out "I'll see you in Montreal (the next Olympic Games) and I'll kick your butt!"

Pre's coaches echoed Newnham's message to Pre; that he had given everything he could. He didn't run for the silver or bronze - saving his energy simply to get *a* medal - but, as always, he gave it his full out effort. On that particular day, at that particular time, Pre had run the best race he could, with bravery and heart. No one, not even those who were not Pre fans, could say he lacked for courage. No one could claim that the 5000 meters wasn't one of the most exciting races ever run. The kid from Coos Bay had made a lasting impression.

Steve stayed on alone in Germany for some time after the Olympics. He had a lot of things to think over. The young man who never seemed to stand still had been brought to a screeching halt by his own doubts. There is a time in the life of every person when he or she faces some dark days. We all wonder about our abilities, our futures, and how to go on after a major disappointment.

When Steve returned to the States, to his trailer with Pat Tyson, his friends, family and fans, he wasn't sure what he was going to do. He had dreamed of running for the gold ever since he'd been a kid in junior high. He was like one of the fishing boats of his hometown, drifting farther away from the familiar Coos River and out into the endless, lonely Pacific Ocean. The water carrier needed to find his anchor. Even someone with utter belief in himself will be forced to confront times of doubt. It's all a part of being human, part of the journey.

Two days after the race, I sat in Skinner Butte Park and I wrote Pre a letter.

Dear Steve,

We don't know one another very well, but that doesn't matter. What I want to say is that I will remember you and the courageous race you ran in Munich for the rest of my life. I'm certain that my thoughts and feelings are shared by so many people here in Oregon and elsewhere; people you may never have met. We all know that you will have your gold. But, more importantly, bear in mind that you have inspired us. You have helped me to see how important dreams are. They are not just fanciful hopes, but realities waiting to happen if we are willing to work hard (and have the guts!)to achieve.

Thank you for showing me that. Having chronicled your achievements, I'm not so scared to dare to reach for some of my own dreams.

I'm proud to say that I have seen you run, work, and give of yourself to others. You should be proud of all your accomplishments too.

Respectfully,
Owen Morgan

I didn't mail that letter. You don't know how many times over the years I wished I had. I wanted to tell Steve how much I respected and admired him, but I felt as though I didn't want to intrude on what was one of the most difficult times in his life. Words were everything to me, and if I wasn't able to put down the exact words that expressed how I truly felt, then I would have failed. It's funny isn't it? There I was, so in awe of Steve's fearlessness, and I couldn't bring myself to mail him a letter to tell him so.

I reassured myself that there would be time. I would mail the letter eventually, or I might pluck up the courage to try and talk with him. I just wasn't ready to do that yet. So I sealed the letter and put it in my "treasure box" which held the few items most dear to me. I continued to hope to see Steve run again, and I wondered how he was feeling, what he was thinking. I waited.

Steve adopted a puppy from a local shelter to be a third roommate in the trailer. Steve's responsibility to Lobo was comparable to the attention needed by a child. Steve had to teach Lobo, feed him, and be close by to provide love and care. He took this duty very seriously. Lobo and his new companion became fast friends.

During the bleak months after the Olympics, Steve was comforted by his animated, four legged buddy. It was at this low point in his life that Steve embraced the most important lesson that coach Bowerman had prepared him for; the greatest challenge was in his loss, and how he was going to pick himself up and carry on now that he was back home. Steve was still living on food stamps, his bank account was low, and he was working at the Paddock to try and make ends meet. I'm sure everyone who has had the benefit of a companion animal knows what a comfort their unconditional love is. That's the one-of-a-kind quality animals possess. You see, Lobo didn't care that Steve placed fourth, or how much money he had in his wallet. As long as the dog could chase after Steve on a run, or feel his ears flop in the wind while sitting in the passenger seat of Steve's car, Lobo was in doggie heaven. Steve too was finding peace and a deeper sense of himself as a person, not just an athlete.

Steve was like a butterfly emerging after a period of stillness, silence and growth. His outward appearance was a sign of the significant changes that had taken place inside. And, like a butterfly, he shed his gossamer cocoon to take on the radiant colors of a changed, free being. Steve's hair was longer, his mustache thicker and he grew side burns. He wasn't going to concern himself with what others thought or expected of him. He had matured. The little pirate had walked through the fire and endured its heat. In so doing, he had captured its energy and brightness to make it his own once again. Steve had indeed picked himself up with grace and dignity.

He could have stayed at his job at the Paddock and concerned himself with making his life a little easier. Who would have blamed him for that? So many of us, after giving what we believe to be our best effort and then feeling as if we have fallen short, simply give up. We walk away using that tired old excuse "I did my best and look where it got me!" What we are really expressing is that we are too scared to try again for fear of being hurt once more.

Coach Bowerman impressed upon Steve the fact that he could make a difference in the lives of many kids. Steve could not and would not walk away from that responsibility. He returned to the University of Oregon for his final semester in 1973. Besides earning a degree in Communications, he set an American record in the six mile, ran the best ever college distance double, and became the first to win four NCAA 3 mile titles (seven NCAA titles in all for his collegiate career) He also set nine collegiate track records and never lost a race more than a mile in length.

I mentioned a little sporting goods store in Eugene called Nike; well, by 1973 the store was slowly growing into a revolutionary track shoe company. The fledgling business was only a year old when Pre was hired to work for his former coach and co-founder, Bill Bowerman. The other co-founder of Nike was also a former U of O track athlete by the name of Phil Knight. Pre was given, or rather gave himself- the title of National Public Relations Manager.

Every revolution needs a visionary and, for Nike, that was Pre. He raised the bar for the company. He had always demanded high levels of excellence in himself, and he now applied the same standards to those creating the shoes. Pre was always after Phil to be innovative and improve the products for the entire running community. When Pre joined Nike, the company had yet to turn a profit and the National Public Relations Manager was paid not in money, but with shoes.

While working for Nike, Pre was reunited with a man he had met briefly during his high school years. Geoff Hollister was a few years older than Pre. Geoff will never forget the impression the then Marshfield student made on him. Geoff was taken by young Pre's confidence and the way in which he approached running.

"Steve was an incredible student of the sport. He asked a lot of questions and pored over books about running."

Spending so much time together at Nike, Geoff and Steve became like brothers. They shared a good deal in common besides running. They both loved cars and architecture, for example. Geoff was married with a young son and home of his own. Pre was maturing, and these were pieces of a life he had begun to wish for as well. The two men had a lot to talk about during their adventures together.

Geoff observed that Pre recognized the beautiful balance in running; which is the fact that a person is bound to get better as the years go by, provided that the person persists in the effort to improve.

Pre was committed to continually improving the prospects of all runners, not just in the standard of their equipment, but also how and where they trained. He was greatly impressed by the unique trails he saw while touring Europe, particularly in Scandinavia. The terrain was much different than anything in the US. The Europeans made use of natural surfaces such as wood chips, dirt trails, and gravel. Running the dunes and beaches of Coos Bay had taught Pre the value of a more organic work-out and he drafted the blueprints for similar trails in Eugene.

He met with the town's officials to construct a trail through Alton Baker Park. Pre, along with Geoff and another Nike representative, designed a fitness center (The Decathlon Club) to be built near the park. The center would offer various activities in addition to running. Pre was closely in touch with the people he met while he was out and about doing his talks and clinics for Nike. Participants told Pre of their fitness needs and wants. Although he was a world-class athlete, Pre did not dismiss anyone who spoke with him about their passion for sports. His two ideas for the trail and the club were just the beginning of what he believed he could accomplish, not just for the people of Oregon, but for all athletes no matter what their level of ability.

But, as with most things that are worthwhile in life, Pre had to fight for his creations. The Parks Advisory Committee - the agency with the power to give the green light on the projects - was very slow in doing so. Pre was already battling the authoritarian ways of the AAU; he'd had enough of this kind of repressive system.

He continued to work with kids, speaking in schools. He and Geoff traveled to various communities to speak to the kids. Pre worked with groups of youngsters by hosting running clinics and one-on-one tuition. He taught them about the true spirit of competition. He spoke of the artistry of the sport and how the struggle to go beyond the average effort transforms the sport into a work of art.

If Pre possessed the heart of a lion, his spirit was that of an artist. Few people ever noticed him rambling alone quietly with his camera, taking pictures. Although he loved the crowded, noisy stands of Hayward Field, the artist in him responded to the peace he could find in nature, away from the grueling hours of training and competition.

He enjoyed being an observer of the natural world. His black and white pictures were of the solitary beauty he saw all around him. As an athlete he was utterly focused on the time and the mechanics of his own body. As a photographer he could focus his lens on the workings of nature; on the trees, the grass and the sky. Perhaps he understood that pictures are a way to preserve a point in time. Running had him always fighting the minutes, trying to overtake them. His pictures were a way of standing still and appreciating the splendor of one split second.

He saw life as a gift and counseled the kids never to waste a moment or to take their talents and skills for granted. He would show them by example, just as he always had; this time a little older and wiser.

This is what enabled Pre to walk tall again after Munich. He may not have been aware of all those people who still and always would support him, but he did know his own heart; a heart that beat in time to a stop watch and the music only he could hear as it pounded within his chest while running the beaches and woods, training harder than ever before. Pre was becoming a man, and time was on his side. The passing of time would give him the ability to climb higher and reach further. He would be able to envision even more breathtaking colors to paint the sky and add more complicated notes to his unique song.

In 1973 Pre claimed 13 first place titles in races which included the mile, 2 mile, 3 mile, 3,000, 5,000 and 10,000 meters. In June of that year he took part in a Restoration Meet to raise money to rebuild the dilapidated west grandstand of Hayward Field. Pre was running in open rebellion of the AAU. He also convinced another world class amateur runner, Dave Wottle, to join him. Pre and Dave were supposed to be embarking on an AAU tour of Africa and Europe, and saying no to the AAU was not really an option. But Pre was tired of being told where he should run and forced to continue to make more money for the already stuffed pockets of the AAU, while he and other athletes continued to live in poverty. It seemed to him that Hayward Field needed his help more than the AAU; so he decided that was where he would be, not in Africa as was expected.

Pre coaxed Dave Wottle to race in Eugene, promising that they would attempt the one mile world record together. He guaranteed Wottle a great time by offering to set the pace and run with Dave all the way. Dave was flattered by the offer. He liked the idea of being free from the AAU's choke hold and the opportunity to run for a world record with the ultimate pace setter, Steve Prefontaine.

In a matter of five days, the meet organizers put together an exciting series of races and packed the stands once again. "Pre's People" came out in droves to see him run in their midst, laying to rest any fears Pre might have had about disappointing those who had supported him. I can tell you, we were ecstatic for the chance to see Pre on the track, and we let him know it with our thunderous applause and chants of the two words we would never forget "Go Pre!"

Pre led the race, but we all knew Wottle was coming. He passed Pre on the back strait. Pre didn't give up so easily; that unyielding sense of fight pulsed through his whole being as the blood did through his veins. He hung in there to challenge Wottle before Dave shot out like the kicker he was for the win. He just missed the world record, finishing in 3:53.3. Pre was a second behind, finishing with a lifetime best. He knew that Wottle was the finest 800 meter runner at that time, and yet Pre still set himself up for the race. He offered Dave the very best in competition; and although Pre wanted to win, he accepted his loss, grateful for his friend's support and for the jubilant crowd that appreciated a thrilling race. Dave and Pre took a victory lap together as their way of showing gratitude to each other and the spectators. Most importantly the Restoration Meet was a highly successful fundraising event.

Dave Wottle recalls the sense of pride he had when he and Pre rejoined the AAU tour already underway. As he and Pre walked into a team meeting, Dave said he felt a bit like the rebel Pre, as the two had shown the AAU it wasn't so all-powerful. Both men, although reprimanded for their disobedience, were allowed to continue on with the tour.

I told you that Pre always "walked the talk". September of 1974 was a perfect example of what I mean. During a "tune-up mile" in preparation for a trip to Europe, Steve was intending to run a sub four minute mile. There were only supposed to be a handful of people in attendance. It was an unadvertised event - just Steve and some of the Oregon Track Club members; but close to a thousand people came out to watch. Steve was warned that the nearby grass seed farmers were burning their ground cover after the harvest in a practice known as "field burning day". The smoke in the air would make it very difficult to run hard. But Steve had said he would do it. He wouldn't break his word and disappoint the crowd. So he ran a mile in 3:58.3. Afterward, he coughed up blood! He didn't spend time feeling sorry for himself, but instead took up a bullhorn and thanked the people who had turned out for their support.

That same year Pre set five American records, one at the World Games in Helsinki, Finland. He also ran in the *only* race he could not finish due to torn stomach muscles.

Pre became more outspoken about the AAU. The organization claimed he was in violation of several of their sacred codes because he was working for Nike (receiving mostly shoes and clothing as pay), and threatened to strip him of his amateur status. He wasn't going to sit back and allow such inferior treatment of himself and his fellow athletes. He understood that with his popularity came responsibility. People would listen to him and he spoke up, whenever and wherever he could. He meant to educate the American public about how their amateur athletes - the very ones who represented the country in the Olympic Games - were being treated. It was important to Pre that Americans not forget about the athletes during the three years they were training devotedly for the Games. He made it clear to the public that all other nations treated homeland athletes with more respect and appreciation.

"I'll tell you," he said in an interview for the Associated Press in March of 1975, "if I decide to compete at Montreal, to make all the sacrifices necessary, I'll be a poor man. If you're not a millionaire, there's no way." Pre clarified his position. "I'm not bitter, I'm outraged. American athletes, especially distance runners, are at a big disadvantage against the rest of the world. We're expected to live by the rules, like not being able to coach, but still train and make our own living."

Pre brought the dirty laundry of the AAU to the attention of his fellow countrymen. He publicly asked the question "Do you think this is right?"

Pre and Pat Tyson said goodbye to their little trailer home on the banks of the Willamette River - no longer college students, but men trying to make their way in the world. Pat took a teaching position in Seattle, but the two former team and roommates stayed connected. Pre would visit Pat in Seattle and once again speak to his students. The earnest twenty three-year-old made a lasting impression on many people in Seattle; one young woman in particular, Laurel James. She was a single mom who rented a basement room to Pat while he settled into his new hometown. Pre's visits and their talks of running sparked something inside Laurel. She decided to take up the sport, but Pre's influence didn't stop there. Laurel opened a running shop called Super Jock and Jill Running Store. It has become something of a landmark in Seattle and today is owned and operated by Laurel's son.

This indeed is what Pre meant about never sacrificing the gift. You see, everywhere you go you can make a difference. You can plant seeds which will grow into strong and lasting creations that may outlive you, but never your spirit. Just like Pre.

Bill Rogers was a teacher living in Boston and looking for work. He once had high hopes of being a successful runner. Bill had been a fine competitor in college. After graduation, he put those dreams aside. But that's the thing about seeds and dreams; once planted, nature takes its inevitable course and something once dreamed of never fully takes leave of a person's heart.

Bill got back into running after a two year break. He surprised a lot of people by finishing third in the World Cross Country Championship held in Morocco, and the running community took note of the relatively unknown man from Boston. If anyone understood the power of encouragement, it was Steve Prefontaine. He wrote a letter to Rogers congratulating him on his accomplishments and offered his assurance that, if Bill stayed the course, he would be a contender for the Olympics.

Pre also sent a pair of Nike running shoes. The shoes turned out to be two sizes too big, but that didn't matter to Bill. He wore the shoes a week after he received them in the Boston Marathon. He had to stop twice in the last few miles to tighten them - much to the puzzlement of the crowd. Bill Rogers became known as "Boston Billy - King of the Roads" that day in 1975. He set a new American and Course Record time of 2:09:55. As far as Pre was concerned, mission accomplished!

Pre bought a house in Eugene. Soon after, his childhood friend Jim Seyler, who had completed his four year military duty and moved to Eugene to begin college, was invited to move in. Pre planted a garden where he grew fresh vegetables for the salads he so loved to eat. Jim lent his hand at helping to build a home sauna from Pre's designs. In order to have enough money to survive, Pre rented a small room above the garage. He also rented one of the other two bedrooms in the house to two brothers who were University of Oregon athletes.

About this time, the newly formed International Track Association made Pre a very sizeable offer to turn professional. This would provide him the money he needed to put into action his plans of opening a sports-themed restaurant - the first of its kind - in Eugene, and have the means to marry and raise children; a lifestyle he had recently been working towards. But there was a down side to this amazing offer; turning professional would mean all of Pre's previous records would be expunged and he would never be able to compete in another Olympic Games.

I was a graduate student at the time, and believe me I know what that amount of income could have done to greatly improve not only Pre's life, but that of his beloved family back in Coos Bay. Pre could finally be free from the unjust demands of the AAU. He could make a life for himself as a runner, supporting himself and his family by doing the thing he loved most. But Pre wasn't one to think in terms of himself only. When he was at Marshfield, he was a pirate among other shipmates. At the University of Oregon, he ran as part of the Bowerman/Dellinger team - a Duck. And as an Olympian, he ran as part of Team U.S.A.

If Pre took the money offered him by the ITA, what would happen to all those other struggling amateur athletes? What would happen if he did not have the chance to go to Montreal and face Lasse Viren for a rematch? These were questions Pre could not allow to go unanswered. He told the ITA to keep the money. He had other, more important, business to tend to. "I run best when I run free," he said. Pre continued on with his crusade to liberate all his fellow runners - his fellow teammates - so they, too, could run free.

Pre shared with a few close friends his doubts about his ability to run as he had before. Despite recent successful races in Europe and the US, he had endured some losses too. But he had made his decision. He would aim for the Montreal Games in 1976. Pre knew that nothing worth dreaming of comes as easily as merely closing your eyes and wishing it was so. Throughout his life Pre had known men in Coos Bay, men like his father, who had persisted through tireless hours of work to achieve the things they wanted.

He was united in heart with the industrious people of his hometown; each one tough, tenacious, and willing to face adversity. It's on the cold, windy, rainy days when few people want to cut wood, run, go to school, or even get out of bed! But it's on those same dreary, miserable days that a person learns the value of taking on the tests before him with fire in his heart. The flame within Pre may have lowered a bit, as when a sudden wind sways the flicker of a candle, but the spark had not gone out. Giving up leaves a person few other options, but getting up after a fall allows for infinite possibilities.

Although a little shaky, Pre got up and proceeded to reclaim his strength and confidence. This meant he had some serious training to do. Former coaches Bowerman and Dellinger would lend their support, as well as Pre's housemate, Jim. I heard that Jim would ride his bike (just to keep up!) with Pre on his daily runs. I think at this point not even Lobo, now a fully grown dog, could keep up with his companion. Pre's focus was as fine-tuned as ever. He had his priorities, had set his course, and was determined to reach his destination; once a pirate, always a pirate.

Pre's aggressive training was paying off. Coach Dellinger said he never saw Pre in better shape. He was ready to take on new challenges. Frank Shorter, a fellow runner, invited Pre to Denver for high altitude training. Some athletes were resorting to questionable practices like "blood doping". They would extract some of their own blood during training and then have it pumped back into their bodies before a race. This gave the body a better way to transport oxygen, thus enhancing performances. Pre didn't want to win that way. He met up with Frank in Denver and the two went on to New Mexico to train at altitudes of 9,000-10,000 feet. There was no flat road running. It was all up and down for 15 to 16 miles a day.

When Frank and Pre were running against gusting winds, being pelted by hardened snow and chilled by freezing temperatures, Pre had to ask his friend what the heck they were doing out there. Frank explained that they were training harder than any athletes in the US. The slightly winded Pre braced himself against the elements, continued on with his run, and never offered another complaint or question.

There was no doubt that Pre was back into his superior, competitive form and in top shape. In fact, the fantastic abilities of his body and mind were scientifically proven. Pre, along with some of the other US superior distance runners, were invited to be part of a study conducted by what was then considered to be the budding new field of sports physiology. The researchers at the Institute for Aerobics Research in Dallas wanted to test the physical and mental capacity of these stellar athletes in order to see what gave them such power.

Pre did not view the experience as a simple collection of data. He saw it as a competition and he was ready to go. The researchers were taken aback by Pre's response in the psychological portion. He said that his main purpose in running a race was not necessarily to win, but to "see who has the most guts." This he meant to demonstrate during the physiological tests.

The researchers considered one particular test to be the best indicator of who had the potential to be among the top athletes in the world - the "VO2 Max test". This test measured the greatest amount of oxygen that can be disbursed to the muscles during physical activity. A score in the high 70s meant that the person was among the world's top runners, a score in the low 80s had only been recorded by a very few cross country skiers and other endurance sportsmen. Each of the runners during the study wanted to score well, but Pre *had* to.

"When he was on the treadmill with the mask over his mouth, fire came into his eyes," Doug Brown, a fellow athlete recalls. "He knew how long everyone had gone on the treadmill and he was determined to go longer."

Pre scored 84-plus. That had only been surpassed by one or two others in the world.

"That test was more a test of will than anything," said Frank Shorter.

Test Pre's will? His determination? They didn't need a treadmill, mask, or any fancy machinery for that. They could have just come out to Hayward Field on race day and watched Pre run. Was Pre one of the most fearless people alive? Well, that was a no-brainer to me and most of us Oregonians.

As I spent my time attending classes and covering various men's sporting events as an intern at a local Eugene newspaper, I had no idea about the plight of women athletes. I'm ashamed to say I was ignorant of the fact that they had no opportunities to advance like their male counterparts. My eyes were opened because of Pre.

Fran Worthen, the incredibly talented Marshfield sprinter, was now looking to enter college herself. Fran was an early pioneer in women's track and field in the state of Oregon. During her time at Marshfield she earned eight individual state titles and two relay titles, contributing to a State Championship for the Marshfield women's team in 1972. She set the National High School long jump record in both her sophomore and senior seasons. Pre continued to work with Fran over the years as a mentor and friend. He tried his utmost to persuade her to run for the University of Oregon as he had. He wanted to make sure Fran could avail herself of the best coaches. But when Fran informed Pre that women athletes were not considered for sports scholarships like men, Pre was incensed. He became very vocal about not only athletes' rights, but women gaining equal rights in the sporting world and all aspects of life.

And, as for Fran Worthen, Pre wasn't letting her off the hook so easily. At age 20 she had told him of her plans to retire from the running game. But Pre had other ideas for his friend from Coos Bay. He was about to take on the AAU in the most brazen act of rebellion of his - or any other amateur athlete's - career.

He had decided to organize a European tour in order to bring the Finnish track and field team to Eugene for a series of meets. He was sure that if he could furnish Lasse Viren with an outing to Oregon, the most memorable site for Viren would be Pre's back as he whipped past him on the track. And he made sure to invite one of the finest female Finnish sprinters so that Fran could be a part of the competition as well. With such an incredible offer, how could she say no?

Planning the Finnish tour was turning out to be much more than Pre had expected. Along with organizing five meets at different locations, including Coos Bay and Eugene, he also had the travel and accommodation logistics to worry about. Athletes and equipment all had to be conveyed from the airport to their lodgings. Geoff Hollister pointed out to Pre that he couldn't just show up at the airport in his MGB two-seater sports car. What to do with all those pole vault poles? And then there was the question of ticket sales, advertising, training and performance schedules, etc.

And, of course, Pre had to battle the AAU. They were not about to give their permission for Pre to host an event that they were not involved in organizing. They sent him numerous letters of warning. The organization threatened that anyone who competed in these unsanctioned events would lose their amateur status and consequently be banned from the following year's Olympic Games in Montreal.

Pre's friends and fellow athletes in Eugene wanted to support his efforts, but they were afraid to give their affirmative about competing. No one wanted to forfeit their chance for the Olympics. Mac Wilkins had his heart set on Montreal. "Macker", as Pre dubbed his teammate, was highly skilled in multiple throwing events - the javelin, discus, shot putt, and hammer. He wanted a chance to challenge the Finnish thrower who had taken the gold in Munich. Pre and Mac had this in common: the unyielding desire to face their opponents once again on home turf.

Mac was also a tad bit envious of all the attention that the brash, blond runner he called "World" was receiving. But he observed and respected how hard Pre gave everything he had to whatever he took on. Macker agreed to take his chances and stand up with Pre against the AAU.

I'm sure if I'd been in Pre's shoes, I would have just thrown my hands in the air and yelled "HELP!" Pre, however, saw this time as an opportunity to become more organized and focused. He started making lists and managed his time more efficiently - he even carried a briefcase. Pre's friends remarked that the experience was a maturing one for him. He was forced to sit still for longer periods of time. He also became familiar with the other side of competition; the business of what goes into hosting a successful event.

Throughout the rocky road of preparations, Pre would not back down from the AAU. Instead he took the occasion and his celebrity status to bring to the public's attention exactly what the organizing body was doing. He held press conferences and spoke openly and honestly about the situation. I was proud to be in the audience and to write about Pre's determined campaign. Pre took a chance, believing that not even the overbearing AAU would keep to its decision once the general public saw how unjustly the athletes were being treated. Pre had faith in his people.

"I don't feel I'm any worse off than I have been in the past. I've caused them probably a lot of embarrassment and a lot of trouble," Pre said of the AAU. "But I'm not trying to get under anybody's skin. I'm just trying to bring the problems to a head and an understanding to make the people of this country realize what's happening in amateur sports. And what's happening is that amateurs do not have the same benefits as, let's say, the Europeans. And I'd just like to bring this acknowledgement to the public."

The AAU backed off and granted permission for the Finnish tour. This would never have been possible had it not been for the outspoken voice of Steve Prefontaine. Unfortunately, this wouldn't be the last time Steve would butt heads with the AAU. He was, however, making great progress in getting the word out about the plight of American amateur athletes.

Before the tour Pre had some other running business to attend to. A month prior to the Finnish meets Pre was set to participate in an Oregon Twilight meet, running in the 10,000 meters. The weather was hardly conducive to running. The wind was like a wall of resistance and Pre was heard saying that he didn't feel much like giving it his all in such nasty weather. Like the AAU, the wind proved to be no match for Pre. He won the race with a world class finish.

May 1975 and the Finnish team arrived in Oregon without any major problems. Pre had learned to delegate responsibilities and allowed his friends to help him see to the details. There was one major disappointment for Pre though. He would not have the chance to race Lasse Viren at Hayward Field, as he had been hoping to do for months. Viren said he could not make the tour because of an injury. Pre felt as if all his work was for nothing. If he could not compete against Viren, there wasn't much to look forward to.

The AAU was up to its old dirty tricks. It had imposed a freeze on athletes' competition. They were permitted to compete in other, non-AAU events only a certain number of days before or after an International AAU event. By doing this, the governing body would compel athletes to be at the AAU Championships and not the all-important European invitational. Pre had decided not to attend the AAU Championships and the international meets. The AAU expressed in no uncertain terms that he would be punished.

Pre was unafraid. Instead he continued to lobby the public for proper assistance for the athletes in his country; assistance that could so easily be gained, like training camps and medical support.

Pre urged his fellow athletes to unite against the AAU. Together they could bring down the outdated organization. Alone, they would continue to be disrespected and treated like puppets. Once again Pre recognized the power of teamwork, of mates banding together.

Pre would not make a profit from the Finnish tour he had arranged, or even compensation for the countless hours of work he had devoted to it. But as the events unfolded, he happily watched the gathering crowds of extraordinary numbers in Coos Bay and the other venues. He experienced the joy of the fans and the gung-ho spirit of the other athletes. Pre was back into his old grove soon enough.

You can bet that I was one of the four thousand people who came out to Pirate Stadium - Pre's old stomping ground, our dear Marshfield High. It was another chilly night, but there could have been a blizzard and the heat generated by all of us in the stands would have incinerated the white stuff. We were packed in together; loggers, mill workers, students, and parents with their children. I was a bit squashed between two burley men, but they were very polite. They tried to offer an apology by saying they were just too excited to sit still.

"I understand," I shouted over the clamor of voices. And I did have a full understanding and appreciation of that exact moment. I felt pride like never before for Coos Bay and her people. I had spent so many years wanting to escape the confines of a small town, thinking there was so much more for me "out there". But being away from this place had only proved that, on this special night, there was nowhere I'd rather be than Marshfield High School with my fellow townspeople. Steve made us all appreciate where we came from, because no matter where the road took him, he never forgot that Coos Bay was his home.

On the bleachers below me a brother and sister who looked to be no older than ten years of age were jumping up and down like pogo sticks. Each had donned a "Go Pre" T-Shirt.

"Ya think we can get Pre's autograph after, mommy?" the little girl asked her mother with breathless anticipation.

"Oh, I don't know, sweetheart. There's a lot of people here tonight, we might not get to see him."

Before any disappointment could settle over the child, I leaned forward and asked "You know what?"

She looked up at me with inquiring blue eyes.

"What?"

"I'm sure that Pre will wait as long as it takes for every kid to get an autograph if they want one."

"Really?"

Her face lit up as if I had presented her a puppy with a bow.

"Really," I confirmed in all seriousness.

"See, Kevin!" She turned to her slightly older brother. "I told ya!"

Their mother seemed uncertain, so I said one more time to assure her "Really."

I may not have known Pre well, but one thing I did know was how much he loved kids; about as much as he loved seeing who had the most guts on the track. It was close to 10PM and we were wired!

What could be better than seeing our pirate back on his own ship, riding the raging storm?

Meanwhile, Pre was blithely predicting to his teammates that he would go for the American record in the 2000. He didn't even know what the record was. He had to ask a fellow competitor, then confirmed he was going for it.

Fellow athlete Dave Taylor said he thought Pre was joking, but when Pre finished the race after commandeering it from his competitors in the last two laps, he had indeed set a new American record with a time of 5:01.4. The stands exploded. After the meet concluded I took my two new friends by the hand, leading them down to the field. They took off like jets and joined the rest of the children huddling around Pre as he went through his warm down. He stayed for a half hour or more signing the kids' programs.

The young girl and her brother triumphantly rejoined their mother and me standing by a fence in the grandstand. Tripping over each other and giggling with delight, they each held up autographed programs.

"LOOK!" they shouted triumphantly.

"Great!" I smiled. My eyes drifted to where Pre was making his way off the field in satisfied tiredness. As he came towards the fence to exit, I caught his glance. I raised my hand (a little too eagerly I feared) in greeting. I'm sure I was smiling ear to ear like a fool. He returned the grin and gave a little salute.

"You know *him*?" the little girl asked in awe.

"Well, no, I..."

It was then I decided I was going to mail my letter. I stood there in Pirate's stadium on that brisk night, flushed with life coursing through my veins; life and its glorious possibilities. I could embrace it all now, because I finally understood how Pre had left an indelible imprint on me. I wanted to be a better, braver person because of him.

"I know that he's a very special man." I said, nodding to the girl.

May 29, 1975. Pre had hoped to leave Lasse Viren in the dust of Hayward Field. Instead, he called on friend Frank Shorter to join in the 5000 race. Frank was training in Eugene at the time and was only too happy to help out and take part. Before the race I spotted Frank and Pre sitting in the grass, chatting and enjoying the company and easy atmosphere of a beautiful spring day. To see them so comfortable together, you'd never know they were about to take to the track as competitors. Pre possessed the wisdom of keeping things in their proper perspective. He could view a man as a true rival on the track, but mere seconds after the race Pre could consider that same man his friend.

The afternoon was warm and splashed with sun, giving a perfect preview of summer. I could hardly imagine those early meets in Coos Bay when the wind would come rushing in from the sea, forcing us to take refuge in jackets and long sleeves.
Pre gave us some unexpected surprises that night. For one thing he wore a black, Italian club singlet, one he'd never worn before (but probably acquired in Europe where athletes traded gear on a regular

basis) and white shorts. He also spent most of the race following Shorter. The audience of around 7,000 was as vocal as ever, but I was beginning to wonder: was Viren's absence aversely affecting Pre?

Not a chance. With three laps to go Pre stepped on the gas and passed Shorter. With his head turned to the side and his eyes closed, Pre's superbly toned body sliced through the finishing tape. He won with a time of 13:23.8, a bit over his own American record. We shouted gleefully, thankful to see Pre doing his thing at Hayward Field once again. This latest win made for twenty five straight victories at races over a mile. He walked a few paces, taking deep breaths before his victory lap, as photographers took advantage of the moment to have the speed demon so near. Pre's face was softer, more relaxed. He seemed rightfully satisfied with his outstanding accomplishment. Speaking to reporters after the race, Pre said he was looking forward to a good summer.

Mac Wilkins had a good night as well. He emerged victorious, beating out his Finnish competition, and gaining more confidence for the Montreal Games. He felt both appreciation and pride for his world famous teammate who was responsible for the unprecedented event.

It was indeed a great beginning of something special, a turning of a page. Pre and his friends posed for pictures with the Finns after the meet. Each person seemed genuinely glad for the rare opportunity; the smiles on all the faces were a testimony to that. Personal wins and losses were not as important as what was achieved as a whole; a group effort resulting in a highly successful athletic event. Pre's determination and grit had proven that the AAU was not as important as it believed itself to be. It was only a matter of time before its disenchanted athletes and their public would deflate the ancient organization's power, like a kid sticking a pin in a balloon.

Pre looked truly gratified. He had been met with a huge amount of opposition along the way, and with those fiery eyes he had stared it down; just like an open track stretched out before him. A new road was rising up to meet him, and he was excited for the journey. The first stop would be Montreal in 1976, and Lasse Viren would be confronted with one heck of a challenge. Steve Prefontaine had faced his toughest opponent, himself. He was the seasoned captain of his own ship now.

5

Early Landing

Pre spent the evening of May 29, 1975 in Eugene, Oregon at a farewell party for the Finns. Many of his closest friends and family were in attendance. Walt McClure, Pre's high school track coach, had even made the trek to join in the celebration. The night was spent talking, reminiscing about times past; of Coos Bay and the tranquil days playing in the summer sun; of endless hours passed on the Indian Ledges and crabbing on the bay - the simple pleasures that define childhood and remain precious forever. Those who were with Pre said he seemed uncharacteristically relaxed, peaceful. The whirlwind of energy was content to stay in one place and be with the people he loved.

Midnight is the time when one day ends and another begins. The past mingles with the present and future, all three brushing against each other like benevolent beings hovering over the earth, their hands clasped together in flight. In these extraordinary moments a lifetime of possibilities exists. The celestial fingers inevitably disjoin as the hands of time move forward. If you look to the sky you will notice that, where there was once a dark patch, a silvery star has taken up residence. Was it always there? Are we now only seeing its light for the first time?

It was in this mysterious hour of transition that Steve Prefontaine drove his sports car down a curving road he had run many times before. The cool breeze slipped its easeful arms around him like a companion, a friend. Pre was no stranger to the wind. They knew each other well. He may have been thinking of family, of Coos Bay, his next challenge, or simply running free.

For reasons that may never be known, he was suddenly forced to swerve his car, veering hard to his left and crossing the center line. Perhaps he was trying to avoid another car invading his path, the headlights blinding him as he made that sharp turn. Pre knew the winding passage - the intersection of Skyline Boulevard and Birch Road - like the back of his hand. But for some reason not of his choosing, he was compelled to train off the familiar trail and slam into a wall of natural rock. His small but heavy car overturned, pinning him underneath - a magnificent, boundless bird stifled by the injustice of chance.

Time was one of the things Pre revered most. When his passionate eyes were fixed on the clock, you might say that it united him to those who had given him life. While driving back to Coos Bay with Pre's father, Elfriede did something she didn't usually do. She looked at her watch and noted the time. It was 12:30AM, and the moment seemed unusually dark. She saw there was an empty space in the sky. Could it be that one spirit, taking leave from the bonds of earth, had stopped briefly to alight on the hearts that proudly stored his love inside - much like the secreted messages hidden away among the rocks of the Butte, the magical writings of children? Pre's name and his message would be written in the sky, and a shadowy patch of hollowness would be filled with the radiant light of a shimmering new star. The person of Steve Prefontaine may have been taken from this world. But his spirit, his legacy, would ride on the wind like the salty drops of the ocean that sprinkled his beloved Coos Bay. Steve was part of the sea and sky, wind and rain; He was part of everyone who stood open-mouthed in the terrible torrent of his passing. We let ourselves be thoroughly drenched by sadness. We needed to be lost in the downpour of grief. There was a strange, uniting comfort in the water.

* * *

There are specific events that stand out in our lives; sad times and moments of great joy; happenings of tremendous significance. No matter how much time passes, we can always look back to those emotion-filled events and recall exactly what we were doing in the moments before and after. The memories are like strands of thread that wrap around our hearts. We can feel their tugging from time to time.

Hopefully, in the case of sad and tragic events, growth and maturity allow us to begin to understand a little more about life and death; and the tugging becomes less painful over time. It still hurts, it always will, but we are able to see the exquisite colors of those threads, grateful for how they tie us to those we have loved and lost.

The shock of Pre's death took its time seeping into our very bones like the chill of winter. How could someone so full of life, someone who had just run a brilliant race less than 24 hours before, now be gone? It was like being shot full of Novocain; numbness and denial were present in almost every person I encountered. I remember after hearing the awful news on the radio that morning, I went out for a paper. I had this ridiculous belief that if I carried on as usual, then what had happened to Pre wouldn't be true. I felt that with my ordinary actions, I could somehow restore the balance.

I didn't speak to anyone as I walked down the street with my head bowed. I heard people talking; Pre's name was being uttered in a kind of reverence. I hoped my legs wouldn't give out before I reached my apartment. When I made it to the safety of the living room, I could smell coffee brewing. I'd started a pot, like I always did, before I went for my paper. That's what's imprinted in my memory: the pungent scent of coffee as I unfolded the front page and encountered Pre's luminous eyes staring back at me.

My knees buckled and thankfully the couch behind me provided a soft landing space. The expression on Pre's face - those eyes! They were not the fierce orbs of resolution; neither were they the laughing, mischievous eyes that had met my gaze on more than one occasion. His face appeared so completely open. His stare was focused on a mysterious horizon that only he could see. It was as if he was looking past the little we understood of this world and into something far deeper and more meaningful.

I gripped that paper for hours it seemed. I didn't read the stories about his passing. I just kept studying the picture. I came to find out the photo was taken the day Pre died. It made sense to me then, and ever since I have seen that picture as the embodiment of who Steve Prefontaine was and is. It's all written in the creases around those large, vivid eyes which showed he had laughed much in his lifetime. It's written in the compassionate and knowing attitude of his young, but astute face; showing all the exchanges he'd had with others during his brief but remarkable life. Some experiences had toughened him, but not to the point of apathy. He was gazing into the distance, but also extending a gentle acknowledgement to every face that met his glance.

I was just beginning to wonder why the paper had become spotted with moisture when Michael opened the front door.

"Owen, I can't believe..."

He took a seat next to me on the couch. I brushed him off, lost in my own thoughts.

"My letter..." I remembered the letter I had sent to Pre a week before. It had taken me a year to get up the guts to post it. "Why didn't I mail it sooner?" I cursed my lack of courage. "It's too late now."

"No, Owen," Michael replied. He was the only one I had told about my heartfelt note. "It was just in time."

I looked at him, then to the photo of Pre in the newspaper. "What do you mean?"

"Take what you wrote to Pre - all the things you said that he taught you, and show him you meant what you said." He rested a hand on my shoulder. "Actions speak louder than words, Owen. Pre taught me that, and I didn't even know him," Michael admitted with a smile.

I knew Michael was right even though I didn't want to recognize the tears that were falling from my eyes without reservation. I wasn't ready to say 'goodbye', nobody was.

The funeral for Pre was held at Marshfield High School's stadium in Coos Bay. The prodigy who began as a pirate returned to his ship and was buried in his Olympic uniform. Pre's fellow runners and friends, dressed in their national team warm-ups, carried his casket. Not so long ago Pre had carried our hopes and dreams on his strong, young shoulders as he circled that track. He had demonstrated the power of the gift without hesitation. Now we collectively labored under the heavy weight of our jumbled emotions, but most especially we cast out our hearts to him, like fishermen their lines into the sea. Pre was laid to rest in a Coos Bay cemetery.

The day following his funeral a memorial service was held at Hayward Field in Eugene, Oregon. Two towns, one heart. As those who loved him gave their testimonies - people like Frank Shorter and Coach Bill Bowerman - the clock facing the field was running. They meant to deliver the service in 12:36.0; a world-record time that Pre had said would please him for the three mile.

As the last minute ticked away the gathering of 4,000 were on their feet cheering one last time for Steve Prefontaine. They saw his fire as he rounded the turn, out in front; eyes locked onto the clock as he whipped by like the wind. He crossed the line in triumph, the clock stopped and the image of a jubilant Pre waving to his people as he breezed by in a victory lap wove itself seamlessly into the air. The people yelled "Go Pre!" for the final time at Hayward Field. Some said the reticent sun pierced its way through the cloud cover as it so often did when Pre ran there.

Eventually the stadium emptied out, its occupants filled with disbelief as if in suspended animation. But out on the track four adolescent girls began to run. One girl, obviously the youngest and smallest of the group, pressed on, even when one of her companions had slowed to a stop. The little one wasn't the fastest or the biggest, but she continued her pace until she completed the round; a feat that would have made Steve Prefontaine proud.

As time moved on, our individual expressions of sorrow became a collective desire. We were stronger, wiser, each with a story to tell - a story of a man who had curled himself into a corner of our hearts, changing our view of the world forever.

During the weeks, months, and years after Pre's death many memorials, tributes and testimonies were given. Countless people demonstrated with their actions and words how much Steve Prefontaine had meant to them, and the gift he had bestowed not just on those who knew him, but on the generations that came after.

* * *

Alton Baker Park in Eugene, Oregon is now the site of the special woodchip running trial that Pre had fought for during his life. The five mile trail was approved the day after Pre's death. You can see runners there each and every day.

Eugene, Oregon is also the site of the annual Prefontaine Classic where some of the world's most elite runners compete.

Coos Bay, Oregon hosts a memorial 10K run every September in Pre's name. Its trail is along one of the same training routes that Pre ran often during his life. A monument stands proudly on the waterfront detailing Pre's achievements.

The Coos Bay Art Museum proudly displays a Prefontaine memorabilia collection housed in beautiful wooden cabinets lovingly built by Pre's father, Ray.

The Prefontaine Memorial Run Committee awards college scholarships to Coos County students who show outstanding contributions, not just in their sport but to their studies and local communities as well.

The location of Pre's accident in Eugene has become a place of pilgrimage for runners and everyone touched by Steve Prefontaine. "Pre's Rock" is a special site where people leave tokens of appreciation. On any given day you can find various track medals, race numbers and ribbons, running shoes, flowers and poems; expressions of love.

Larry Norris with the Oregon Track Club was inspired by Pre. He also ran with the inmates at the Oregon State Penitentiary. Larry was asked by the prisoners to arrange for a bronze plaque to be erected at Pre's Rock on their behalf; the men who Steve had worked with so devotedly.

The inmates had saved their money over the years from various track meets they held and from the little bit they made from prison allowances. Larry agreed to help in this labor of love and proceeded to Eugene Granite and Marble Company to arrange for a small plaque. Upon hearing Larry's story, the company decided to donate the entire cost of the memorial - several thousand dollars.

They created an exceptional, polished stone from a special South African marble containing flecks of gold.

Larry also obtained permission from photographer Brian Lanker to use that haunting picture of Steve taken on the day of his passing. The result was a stunning memorial including a dedication, printed in beautiful gold lettering, which the inmates composed themselves.

"PRE"

For your dedication and loyalty
To your principles and beliefs...
For your love, warmth and friendship
For your family and friends...
You are missed by so many
And you will never be forgotten...

The money the inmates had collected was used to purchase the stone upon which the memorial sits. It was imperative for these men to express the fact that they would never forget the generous athlete and incomparable man who had not forgotten them.

I took Michael's advice and vowed to live the lessons Pre had taught me. I traveled the world to report on athletes. I chronicled many who had also taken Pre's message to heart. Some had the benefit of knowing him; some simply tried to follow his supreme example. Great athletes like Bill Rogers, Alberto Salazar, Mary Decker Slaney, Todd Williams, to name a few. Some people who are inspired by Pre are running right now; track coaches, junior and senior high school students, college scholars, and some who have yet to be born.

Pre's example and encouragement spurred on women athletes to continue their fight to gain support for their cause over the following years; women like Pre's friend, Fran Worthen. While in college she trained with the men's track team. This provided a springboard to many national meets. She was a finalist in the 100 and 220-yard dashes and the long jump, and won the National Championship in the 220 in 1974. That same year she competed for the US in the short relay against the USSR at Duke University, and the team set an American record.

Mary Paczesniak started on the volleyball team at Oregon State for 4 years and played in the first two *ever* National Intercollegiate Volleyball Championships for women, placing 10th the first year and making it to the national quarterfinals the next. She also won the Pacific NW doubles championship in tennis.

Both these Coos Bay natives knew what it meant to fight for individual and team rights because they knew Pre. And both these women went on to work with kids as coaches and teachers - just like Pre.

Perhaps no one knows that fighting spirit better than Pre's little sister Linda. The young girl who skate-boarded, climbed the Indian Ledges, and learned how to drive a stick shift car with her beloved brother, achieved many successes of her own. Linda graduated from Marshfield in 1971, where she played on both the basketball and tennis teams for four years. She was District

Champion in doubles for three years, accomplishing something no other woman had in the past. She was the quarter and semi-finalist for State. In college, Linda was an MVP and team captain, and claimed championships in singles and doubles once again. After graduating from the University of Oregon, she took up the game of racquetball with great success. She won the Oregon Singles Championship in 1978 and was National Singles Runner-up. Steve's sister joined the Women's Professional Racquetball tour and competed for three years. When Linda left the tour, she was the 6th ranked player in the country. She taught racquetball for twenty years.

Today Linda generously gives of her time to speak about her big brother giving her unique perspective as to who Steve was as a person and an athlete. She is an accomplished woman in her own right, but it's very important to Linda to keep the fire of Pre burning bright.

I became less afraid to use my gift to speak out with my words and cover the important issues. One of my proudest moments came in 1978. A great story was breaking - the Amateur Athletic Act had become law. The ancient and useless AAU was forced to disband. Amateur athletes were finally granted their rights.

Stories were written about US distance runners defying the International Amateur officials in 1981, and bringing about the professional status for the sport of track and field.

These watershed events would never have been possible if not for the grassroots efforts, tireless devotion, and the forthright influence of Steve Prefontaine. It's not an overstatement to say that all athletes who came after owe a debt of gratitude to Pre. The world of athletic competition is changed for the better because of him.

It's no surprise to me that, of all the athletes who have represented Nike and worn its gear, the company created a statue of only one. The bronze likeness stands at their Oregon Corporate headquarters; that of Steve Prefontaine.

6

Circling the Earth
Pre's Gift

It seems I have come to the end of my story about Steve Prefontaine, but not really. You see, Steve's time here among us may have been all too short, but being the focused and dedicated man he was, he didn't waste a moment. Steve made sure that those he loved knew it (with his great, big bear hugs!) and those he felt needed help and guidance received it.

I never doubt that Steve's spirit, his essence, is still circling the earth. All I have to do is walk the dunes of Coos Bay, or take a trek through the perfumed woods. I can stand in the bleachers of Hayward Field, or I can look to the sky and watch with anticipation as a dark spot is suddenly and gloriously illuminated by a single star. Who Steve was, what he worked and fought for, continues to be present in every child, every person who believes he or she can be better and give more.

I hope this story will mean something to you. Perhaps you will think of Steve during a difficult moment - a moment, maybe, when you feel as if what you wish for most is not worth the effort and you're considering giving up. I hope you will think of Steve then and give yourself the benefit and challenge of time. I hope you will give yourself one more mile. But don't just take the word of one person; listen to some of the voices who knew Steve best, and those who know of his lion's heart.

Pre believed in perseverance and being rewarded for hard work. He believed in pursuing your goals to the fullest.

Kirk Gamble
Former Marshfield Track Team Member

Steve's message would be to never give up. He was just a scrawny little kid who decided he wanted to run. He became one of the best in the world.

Elaine Finley Giannone
Friend

Pre believed that if you set your mind to something, you would be surprised at what you can do. Pre set his goals high and went for it.

Fred Girt
Fellow Marshfield Track Team member

It didn't matter who he was running against, Pre was able to go beyond the limits. He gave 110% all the time.

Stan Goodell
Track and Field coach

May 30, 1975. As I went outside, I knew this was a day that Pre would have loved. It was late spring, a little cloudy but it was warm with the promise of warmer temperatures to come. This was a day that the people of Eugene would see Pre putting in his road work. Sometimes you'd see him near Alton Baker Park, and other times you'd see him along a Eugene street running at an incredible pace — a Pre pace. I knew then that I'd never see Pre run again. I knew I'd never see him in the Olympics, running against (and beating) Lasse Viren. I knew it was truly the end of an era that would always be remembered... and it was. But you know what? Pre would never have us think about his death. He'd want us to think about living our lives in a way that we'd leave this planet in a better condition than we found it. If we saw injustice, he'd want us to stand up against it. He'd want us to make our voices heard over world problems. Pre was small in stature but huge in heart. He'd never let anything beat him.

Tracy Hickman Esq.
Former Spencer Butte Jr. High Student.

If you defined Bowerman as 'the great teacher' and Pre as 'the great student', you would have an example of the mentor and the pupil. Bill (Bowerman) said, 'Find something you love to do and dedicate yourself to it.' Pre (and the rest of us) heard that, but Pre really got it.

Geoff Hollister
Friend
Nike Representative

I knew Pre from the time he first started to run and showed a lot of promise. I remember the race at District, his sophomore year where he finished third and didn't qualify for State. I recall how confident he was going into that race that he was going to qualify for State, and how devastated he was afterward. From that time on, I don't think he ever lost another high school race. He had talent, but his work ethic was unequalled. I saw many of his races throughout high school and most all of his races at Hayward Field. The thing that I will always remember is the supreme effort he always gave. He wasn't afraid to run against superior runners in events that weren't best suited to his talent; but when he did, his competitors always knew they had to run their best to beat Pre. His races were tremendously entertaining to watch because he always gave everything he had to give. You don't see that much in track and field today, as most world-class athletes seem to avoid running against other top runners as much as possible.

Bob Huggins
Family Friend
Prefontaine Memorial Committee

When people ask me how to describe Steve, you have to talk about 'tough'. You can accomplish a lot by being either mentally tough or physically tough. There's practically no limit if you're both...Pre was both! He wrote the book on "tough!"

Tom Huggins
Friend
Marshfield track team member

I came to the Department in 1983. In the early seventies my father was in charge of the Recreation Yard (of the Penitentiary) and brought many notable Oregon athletes into the prison, including Mr. Prefontaine. I recall my father's excitement of world class athletes coming to the Penitentiary to share their experiences and techniques.

When I began my career in Corrections, the running program was still going strong with six races a year, all culminating in an October marathon with almost all the internal gates of the prison being opened up for the runners. Oftentimes we had over 100 guest runners at the marathon. The event offered running shoes and apparel as prizes and was sponsored by Make-A-Wish and Nike. The growth of the program and the involvement of the sponsors was no doubt related to the involvement of Steve Prefontaine and other Oregon runners.

During my days at the Penitentiary, the inmates still talked fondly of Mr. Prefontaine and all seemed to have been inspired by his presence and willingness to help. Since the early seventies, running has been a long established avenue to both physical and emotional health for inmates.

Randy Geer
Emergency Preparedness / Central Mail Administrator
Oregon Department of Corrections

Pre was so intense in whatever it was he was doing. He felt that whatever time he had here he had to get it done. He didn't waste time and he took things that were important to him very seriously.

Walter McClure
Former Marshfield High Head Track and Field Coach
Prefontaine Memorial Committee

I think as we grow up, it is important to find our special talents or abilities and make the most of them. Pre found that he had a talent for running and a mental toughness that made him hard to beat on the track... Even though he died at a young age, he has made his mark on thousands of young people and is still influencing young and old alike today. Find something you enjoy and are good at, and work at it to make a difference in the world, like Pre did.

Larry Norris
Oregon Track Club

To me, Pre's message was 'anything is possible if you are true to yourself.' If you have a love for something and strive to achieve your best, you can get your dream. Don't give up!

Mary Paczesniak
Former Marshfield athlete
Teacher

Steve exemplified tenacity - tenacity in racing, in training, in causes, in life. It was that tenacity which endeared him to his teammates, competitors, coaches, family, even spectators. And it was that tenacity which continues to fuel his legacy even beyond the athletic world. The world knows him as Pre. I knew him as Steve - a young athlete who picked himself up from disappointment to shatter barriers: barriers of doubt, of records, of traditions, of organizations, of world strife, of relationships. Yet even as a hard charger, he never failed to have time for the smallest fan or that young rookie coach.

Phil Pursian
Former Marshfield High Track and Field Coach

Everyone knows how much Steve loved a challenge, but what some may not know was his playfulness. I counted both on his grin and the twinkle in his eye when he worked with junior high kids. He loved our House mascot, the scorpion; because a scorpion doesn't go looking for trouble, but if someone messes with it, watch out! And Steve wasn't afraid to ask questions. He knew a person had that right. He was fearless in everything he did and that, coupled with his keen sense of justice, made him formidable. Go Scorpions. We Shal.

Ray Scofield
Former Teacher (House 34 Adviser)
Roosevelt Jr. High School

Pre felt it was important to have goals, to be yourself and not to be afraid of what others may think of you.

Tim Wall
Fellow Marshfield High student

Pre was a person who wanted to give back. He wanted kids to aim for greatness and not just settle for average. He encouraged kids to be their best because Pre felt every child had a gift. And when they found what that was, they should work hard at it.

Fran Worthen
Friend
Marshfield Track and Field Coach
Prefontaine Memorial Committee

I remember when I first really got into track, probably in eighth grade or so, my dad showed me the movie 'Prefontaine'. He said Pre was 'the man' when he was in high school and that I needed to see this movie. All in all, I've probably seen 'Prefontaine' over a hundred times. In middle and high school, I watched the movie before every race. There was something about Pre that was inspiring and really got me excited to compete. I was in awe of his determination and daring racing style. It was something I wanted to emulate in my own running.

John Richardson
Runner
University of Kentucky alumni

I think of the painful times in running and I just remind myself that Pre was a man who made pain an aspect of life.

Connor Kasler
Runner, Student

When I first read the book PRE (The Story of America's Greatest Running Legend) by Tom Jordan, I was so moved. I wanted to be that type of runner - the runner who literally runs his guts out on that track. Pre was not a 'sit and wait' guy. He laid it out there and really made races. This is what I believe in today... All of the things that Pre has been quoted saying have touched me. All his races, his determination, his perseverance, his belief in himself, and his stubbornness has helped me become a more focused runner. I really can't explain the magnitude of his influence in my life. Pre believed in what he did, he believed in challenging himself as well as his opponent. I strive to be half of what Pre was.

> Jamie Geissler
> Runner
> University of Florida student

Everything I see in Pre inspires me. He overcame all odds and doubts to be the best. He never gave anything less than his best, and I remember that when I run a race, but no one could do it better than Pre

> Chris Cline
> Runner, student

Pre said "A lot of people run a race to see who is the fastest, I run to see who has the most guts." I was born running. It was a natural occurrence for a farm kid, the runt of the litter with domineering older brothers. If I wanted to keep up, I was running. If I wanted to get away, I was running. After years of sweating through a multitude of community runs, Junior Olympics races, Hershey track meets and junior high sports, I joined the high school cross-country team. By this time I was no longer running to get somewhere or away from something. I was running because it made me feel whole inside. It was beautiful and it was love... Each day became a race to see how strong I was, how tough I could be, how much guts I truly had. I didn't even need other people anymore, thrashing myself was enough of a challenge.

> Annyika Corbett
> Runner, student
> Recipient, Prefontaine Memorial College Scholarship (2006)

It was Pre's eyes that spoke to me as a runner. The poise and willpower of his stare. No trace of uncertainty, only strength of mind. That is why Pre was the first, and the last.

Brett Holts
Runner, University of Oregon alumni
Nike Youth Running Coordinator

I became a runner when I moved to Oregon. I'm not sure whether my family's relocation to the Coos Bay/North Bend area, Distance Mecca and hometown of Steve Prefontaine, or some other factor that prompted this transformation. However, to my then fourth-grade brain, the two were indistinguishable... I was hooked, and I have been running ever since. Running is not as glamorous or as high profile as many other sports. However, the inherent simplicity of an individual striving not necessarily for victory, but for a personal goal renders running unique. For me, nothing is more beautiful than the passionate pursuit of something loved. It is the effort that is beautiful, not just the outcome.

Kassy Lynass
Runner, student
Recipient, Prefontaine Memorial College Scholarship (2006)

As a high school runner, a lot of kids have asked me about Pre because they see all the advertisements. I don't know what to say when they ask. How can you explain something that even today people are trying to figure out? There are kids that want to be like Pre on every track team across America, but not very many kids are willing to suffer and make the sacrifices he did. I will most likely never be the best runner in the world, and that's OK, because the

*things I have learned from Pre are so much more important to me;
as a son, brother and friend, because you cannot run forever! But
you can always give nothing less than your best.*

Dylan Hatcher
Runner, Student

*My junior track season at Mead High School was in 1996.
In years passed, Coach Tyson had organized a week long trip during
our spring break to travel down to California to race at one of the
most competitive high school track invitationals -the Arcadia Invite.
That year, our spring break didn't coincide with the invite and we
couldn't make the trip. The team was disappointed, but true to
Tyson's ability to improvise and inspire, he developed a new trip
which he dubbed "The Oregon Adventure." It was to be a
journey to live and train as Pre had. And with a group of ten guys we
made our way from Spokane to the Oregon coast.*

*We spent two days running the beaches of Newport with former
Mead runners and University of Oregon All-Americans who told us
stories of Prefontaine running at the college level. I think we were all
seeing life in Oregon's green and gold at that time. We spent another
day training in the sand dunes between Florence and Coos Bay - a
place Tyson said Pre used to do long runs. The scenery was beautiful
and sparse. We trained hard.*

*On the fourth day we drove into Coos Bay, Pre's hometown and
birthplace of his legend. Our first stop was the cemetery where he
was buried. Tyson, not knowing where the tombstone was after so
many years, suggested we walk around to find it. Ten high school
boys have never been so reverent. I was the first to find the*

gravestone. On it is a quote which captures Pre's spirit and deserves to be read only in person - part of the pilgrimage I'll preserve. We all gathered in silence. All week we were training in the shadow of his legend. Tyson taught us not only about Pre's fantastic athletic achievements but about his character, that unique drive and passion toward personal excellence and extremes. Coach Tyson then took us to Pre's parents' house - Ray and Elfriede - where we sat on the floor and listened to them describe his childhood, his mischief, his work ethic, his dedication to his team - his community.

As a final stop on our journey, we drove to Eugene and the University of Oregon. On a Friday night at 8:00 PM we all assembled on the storied track where Pre had run so many incredible races. We were warmed up for a one mile time trial, the culmination of our week of training and indoctrination into Prefontaine experience. Current U of O athletes came to watch, as did Pre's college and Olympic coach, Bill Dellinger. The track was dark and very quiet as we started save the small audience of alumni and coaches. I have never been on a track so quiet. Most of us ran to a personal best time that night. No competition, no crowded bleachers, just a great week of living with Pre as our coach had.

> Morgan Thompson
> Former Mead High School Student. Runner
> Spokane Washington

Pre has inspired me by taking the emotions of being made fun of at the early part of his life and working through them to fuel his desires to run like a rebel.

> Jason Arbour
> Runner, student

Pre is a true inspiration to high school athletes today, especially here at Mead where we have been blessed with a coach who knew him. Pre shows runners everywhere that just a regular guy from a small town in Oregon can become one of the greats by using his ability to endure the pain and run even when it hurts and quitting would be so easy. Pre showed the world that all the talent in the world does not matter if there is no desire to win, but when you have the desire- a good runner can become great. Pre is what keeps me going when it seems so easy to quit; just the thought of the pain he endured and how great he became because of the fiery desire he possessed.

> Dan McIntosh
> Runner, student
> Spokane, Washington

Steve Prefontaine continually challenged himself to become a better runner. However, I have found that this same philosophy can be applied to life in general. From this quote ("To give anything less is to sacrifice the Gift.") I now understand that the gift is the opportunity to develop ourselves into outstanding human beings... In Pre's case, he was given the gift of running. By continually giving his best in running, Pre was able to develop himself into a magnificent runner and human being who is still remembered today... Although I did not have the privilege of meeting Steve Prefontaine, his quote has provided me with the inspiration to overlook mediocrity and to relentlessly pursue the development of my life.

> Chris Platanto
> Runner, Willamette University student

Recipient, Prefontaine Memorial College Scholarship (2006)

There is no profound or sophisticated way to put it. Pre is simply an inspiration for not only runners and athletes, but for all people. His unwavering confidence and his ability to make it happen on race day are exceedingly admirable. Pre wasn't afraid of his opponents, but he put the fear of God in those that raced him. That is the type of poise and self-belief young runners strive to possess. Pre set his goals high and forced himself to achieve. I aspire to his competitive nature and his style of racing. He doesn't sit and kick. Pre is far gutsier. He drives himself and his competitors to the limit from the beginning of the race to the tape. After delving into Pre's story, I am dreaming bigger and honoring the gift more than ever.

Lindsay Petri
Runner, University of Kentucky student

From the determined six year old persevering through the home stretch of his first race, to the chiseled Olympian fiercely competing for a gold medal, the grace and power of a well run race is as impacting to me as my first glance at the Mona Lisa... The beauty that Steve Prefontaine strove to portray in his running will forever be a masterpiece hanging in the hearts of those who have witnessed his extraordinary talent... Pre was able to exemplify this unmatchable beauty in its purest form every time he stepped foot on the track. In some small way, I joyfully follow in his footsteps as I explore all the wonderful aspects of running.

Megan Hibner
Runner, student
Recipient, Prefontaine Memorial College Scholarship (2006)

This book and Pre's message are timeless. Pre was the 'blue collar guy' that made a huge impact on those who knew him or were ever connected with his spirit. He was larger than life. I learned a lot from Pre. I learned how to relax and have fun and not take life too seriously. I learned about time management skills as he filled up his day fuller than others. I learned about charisma and how that is huge when you are leading others. I've always been about inclusion not exclusion. Steve lived that attitude as well. He befriended those that were in need. Some say he was cocky, I say he was confident. He walked the talk! He was a 'get things done' kind of guy in everything he did; plenty of examples of that quality throughout the book. Since his death, I've always kept Pre's flame alive in those I've taught and coached. Tom Jordan (author of 'PRE, The Story of America's Greatest Running Legend, Steve Prefontaine'), always called me 'The Keeper of the Flame'. I am proud of that statement by Tom. Pre was so alive, and we really got along. Pre connected with people who were genuine. It's hard to find genuine, hard-working people in the world today. What a message Pre left for all of us.

Pat Tyson
Friend, former roommate
Fellow U of O teammate
Track and Cross Country coach

Last week I called a pressure washer company in Ohio. I needed to order some parts. It was a very typical order. "Yes, you can ship that ground UPS. Yes, the company name is Farr's True Value Hardware, 880 S. First, Coos Bay, OR."

C O O S   B A Y ORYGUN. Then it happened. It's happened before lots of times, again and again. I'm just a hardware store owner in a town of 15,000. That's less than almost anywhere.

"Isn't that where that guy - the runner came from?" I was asked by the person taking my order.

"Yes," I say, "and I'm a product of that guy." My life is a lot of things, but in everything that I am, a little bit of Pre lives.

I've had lots of time to think about it, lots of time to wonder and play "what if?" What if Steve had lived? How would things be different? Would Pre have won that coveted gold metal - that piece of metal that he gave up hundreds of thousands of dollars of professional track salary so that in a simpler, more honest time he could maintain his amateur status to represent his country one more time and take on the world?

I don't know what would be different in the rest of the world. This I can guarantee, Coos Bay would be different. It would be better by his will - his iron will and his energy. Coos Bay, the town that gave Pre his start, nurtured him, beat him up and molded him. HIS town would be different.

For over 28 years - 4 years longer than Pre lived, a small group of Steve's friends and neighbors and some who never knew him have helped to keep his memory a part of Coos Bay. Nike and the U of O, and others have kept his image before the world; but the annual Prefontaine Memorial Run has kept Pre's memory alive in Coos Bay.

I could tell you stories of the families and individuals who appear in Coos Bay every week from everywhere in the world for only one reason, because Coos Bay, Oregon is where the USA's most famous runner grew up.

It's a small piece of Coos County, but it's the only thing that a fellow from Ohio who took my pressure washer parts order knows about Coos Bay. And it's a gift from the life of a very special young man from Coos Bay who dared to think that he could be the best in the whole wide world.

To the billions of people who don't live in Coos Bay, Oregon, I'm the guy from the hometown of Steve Roland Prefontaine!"

> Jay Farr
> Life-long friend and teammate
> Prefontaine Memorial Committee.

Robert Collier was quoted as saying "Success is the sum of small efforts, repeated day in and day out." I can imagine my friend Steve would have stated it a bit differently, something like "Success is the sum of GREAT EFFORT, each and every day." Small efforts didn't exist in Steve's world.

From a very young age, Steve kept a daily journal of his goals and visions. Every day he would write in this journal and remind himself of what he wanted to accomplish and what he had to do to achieve those accomplishments. These writings were not just those of running, they included: getting good grades in school, being a respectful son, brother and friend to those around him.

Steve didn't realize he was a better athlete than most others. You may say how can this be? It's true. He believed that if he worked and trained harder than his competition, he was the only one that could win. So he trained with more vigor and focus than anyone

I have ever known. Pre wanted every young athlete to believe that no matter what their ability, with determination and hard work - really hard work - they could win also and achieve far more than they ever dreamed possible. He wanted every young person to believe in themselves and with every breath and ounce of focus, achieve something they could be proud of.

Remember, during Steve's four years as a student at the University of Oregon, he attended every practice, every day, for Track and Field and Cross-Country. Four years of not missing one practice! Were there days he didn't feel well? Absolutely! Were there days he wanted to goof off with his friends? You bet!

This was the Steve I knew from age 10 until the day he died. His unique energy resembled that of a shooting star; he had a determination like no other, and such perseverance that you would often sit back and look on with wonder and astonishment.

If Steve were with us today (and I often believe he is), he would smile that larger than life mischievous smile and be pleased that his message is being conveyed to all of you.

Jim Seyler
Lifelong friend

See ya, Pre.

We'll take it from here. . .

CPSIA information can be obtained
at www.ICGtesting.com
Printed in the USA
FSHW010547010420
68693FS

9 781435 716292